You Never Know When You'll Get Lucky!

Priyadarshini Narendra has spent several years in the advertising industry, and has many award-winning campaigns to her credit. Many of the hilarious incidents in *You Never Know When You'll Get Lucky* draw from her advertising experiences. An MBA from IIM Kolkata and INSEAD, she has also written a highly successful book published in the UK. Currently, she works as a management consultant and lives with her husband in Delhi in a house spilling with children and books.

Published by
FiNGERPRINT!
An imprint of Prakash Books India Pvt. Ltd.

113/A, Darya Ganj,
New Delhi-110 002
Tel: (011) 2324 7062 – 65, Fax: (011) 2324 6975
Email: info@prakashbooks.com/sales@prakashbooks.com

facebook www.facebook.com/fingerprintpublishing
twitter www.twitter.com/FingerprintP
www.fingerprintpublishing.com
For manuscript submissions, e-mail: fingerprintsubmissions@gmail.com

ISBN: 978 81 7234 400 9

Processed & printed in India at Thomson Press

Praise for the book

"A wonderful first attempt. The characters and the settings spring out of the book, play out in front of one's eyes, and leave a lasting impression. Unputdownable and hilarious."

Durjoy Datta, *bestselling author*

"A book about the inconvenient, unreasonable love we all hope to be consumed by – and about embracing it without fear. A must for cynics of that four-letter word!"

Aastha Atray, author, Mills & Boon's *His Monsoon Bride*

"Witty, intelligent . . . kept me hooked till the end."

Ruchita Misra, author of the bestseller, *The (In)eligible Bachelors*

"[a book about] plodding through many Mr Wrongs to find Mr Right . . . A wonderful ride through the life of a regular girl, negotiating the minefields of the modern urban dating scene."

Kiran Manral, author of *The Reluctant Detective*

"A modern-day story about the quest for that ever evasive true love, quirky workplace situations and characters that regularly land themselves into sticky spots. An entertainer!"

Parul Sharma, author of *Bringing Up Vasu: That First Year* and *By The Water Cooler*

"A racy romp through the other side of advertising - far from the asinine artworks, boring briefs and multitudinous media plans!"

Gautam Bhimani, author, columnist and cricket commentator

FINGERPRINT!

Praise for the book

1

Okay, maybe that wasn't exactly my best move. Why do I get myself into these things? I didn't know the layout of the farmhouse, so I was dodging from room to room, hoping no one spotted me skulking around or, even worse, stopped to ask what I was doing there.

Boy, things were sure on a lavish scale! Marble flooring in the loos and overwaxed Pergo everywhere else. Not the best thing if you're wearing stilettos, like I was. Especially, stilettos with metal tips. It's as it is tough to tiptoe around in them, and with the farmhouse's polished marble, I was literally scrabbling for footing, much like my spitz when he's running around in the house.

I guess when you have this much money, you've got to show it off somehow. Pity, they couldn't buy taste along with all that ostentatious display. The house looked like a bad imitation of Shakaal's den. Crimson, hunter green, cobalt blue and so on—a different colour overwhelming each room. This was coupled with oversized cushions, overstuffed sofas—with either jungle prints or gold tassels or both—and elaborately patterned wool and silk carpets. I wondered if the owners were blind or did they like to have their rooms screaming at them? Every blessed thing that could be was gilt—from picture frames on oversized canvases and lamp shades to door handles. And there was too much of everything, all jumbled up ad nauseum—large crystal bowls cheek by jowl with Lladró, potpourri jars, Chinese porcelain vases. They would be infinitely better off with a little interior editing, I thought. It was almost enough to make me long for the Delhi definition of haute décor—beige! Heck, I was feeling claustrophobic!

Oh ok, I better rewind a bit so that you know who I am and what I'm talking about. I do have a tendency to start my stories in the middle; not a terribly good trait in a copywriter. That's what I do for a living. I'm a copywriter—I write ads in an ad agency. At that time, I lived in Gurgaon, worked in Vasant Vihar and was a twenty-eight-year-old, 5'6", reasonably proportioned (though with a big . . . um . . . derriere) girl, with red-streaked hair, brown eyes the exact colour of clay—☹—and what's known as a 'wheatish complexion'. And at that moment, I was at a wedding with my mom and Bunty, and I was trying to hide from both. I'd even switched off my mobile to avoid them.

See, my mom's mission in life was to get me married off. The day I turned 23, she started with her antics, and with each passing year, she had become antsier. It was the most critical venture in her life, as if she were rehabbing me or something. As for me, well, I was not against marriage, but then it had to be for the right reasons, to the right guy, no? I mean, I couldn't bring myself to get married because "it was time" or in my case "high time". I mean, it is the 21st century, right?

So I'd been going through the usual dating-disasters—you know, meeting all the wrong guys who turn you on for all the wrong reasons at the wrong places and at the wrong time, blah blah. I'd never fallen in love with anyone, though there had been a few 'in-lusts'.

Mom and Dad, of course, had no idea about all that. Mom's big dream had been to get me married off to Bunty, her school-friend Neera Auntie's son. Apparently, all the old movies where they showed parents of newborns making ridiculous pacts to get them married off to each other rubbed off on Mom and Neera Auntie, and they animatedly ended up making a similar pact. Only, Bunty and I couldn't stand each other. Whenever Mom used to be in town, she somehow dragged Bunty into my life and I had a hard time fending him off. Like, at that moment, she'd gotten him to this wedding with her since Neera Auntie couldn't accompany her.

This was a really big, high-society, jumbo kind of a wedding with everything overdone and under-thought. Mom, Neera Auntie and the bride's mother were all in college together, so Mom had come to town to attend the wedding. Thankfully, she was heading back to Meerut the next day. Dad used to be in the army but he had retired some years ago and had started a horticulture business that was not exactly making him Bill Gates. But he was happy doing it, which is what counts.

"There you are!" Mom said, marching up to me and catching hold of my elbow. "Where have you been? I've been looking all over for you. Bunty is also out hunting for you."

"Oh . . . I was just looking for the washroom."

"Good Lord! Can you never go anywhere without having to use the loo?"

"Mom!"

"Shut up! Let's go meet the girl and boy. I want to get this gift off my hands."

Mom, immaculately dressed in a *kanjeevaram sari* and a matching *shawl*, had somehow bullied me into wearing the 'wedding-outfit' she had brought along. As she turned around and started walking towards the stage, I followed her—swishing in my turquoise-blue fish-tail *ghaghra-choli* and oversized *jhumkas*, feeling rather Bollywood-ish.

I have to say, it may not be politically correct but whenever I go to a wedding, I always check if the bride is beautiful and the groom handsome. Don't you? Well, in this wedding I was sadly disappointed. The groom was paunchy as heck and the bride was painfully weighed down by jewellery and a flashy *lehenga*. It must have weighed, what, ten kilos? I could barely see her face; I was so blinded by the shiny, tinsel embroidery on her outfit and the sparkly kilos of gold and diamonds that were heaped on her.

Added to this, the main people in the wedding party—the bride, the groom, the bride's parents and the groom's parents—had decided to wear matching ensembles; all designer stuff, mind you. So their outfits were all purple and neon green. Now, these two colours may look cool on walls, but trust me, when combined with the blingy jewellery and overdone embroidery required by the nouveau riche; they were a pain in the eyes. The farmhouse venue had also been done up to coordinate with these colours, so paler purples and greens were all over the place. If you blinked too hard you couldn't tell where the tents began and where the bride and groom ended.

The food menu did look fantastic though. There were different canopies serving different kinds of cuisines—Mongolian Barbeque, Italian, Szechuan Chinese, Thai, Vietnamese, Mexican, French, Kashmiri, Punjabi, Rajasthani and South Indian. There were separate *chaat* and dessert stands. An amazing blue-green ice sculpture that looked like the RK Films logo was in the midst of the food area.

"Why don't you head for dinner? I see some people from my class in college that I must say hello to. I'll catch you later."

"Okay, Mom."

"If I spot Bunty, I'll send him your way." Seriously, it was like Mom became deaf whenever I told her I was not interested in him!

The buffet line was pretty long. All the stalls were crowded as always by people who had plates full of food in their hands, but who seemed afraid to move away lest it all finished before they were able to refill and then fill again. I picked up one of the super heavy plates for myself and got into the queue. I had just heaped my plate with some yummy-looking goodies when I caught sight of Bunty, looking like he was trying to spot me. I immediately hid behind some guests near me and when this failed, I tried to slink off inconspicuously to a table in one far corner of the ground. I wanted to relish my food in peace.

No such luck. I spotted Bunty coming my way within minutes. I had to do something fast. I looked left and right but there was no place to hide. I panicked! The next thing I knew, I was under the table, clutching my dinner plate!

The purple, green and silver tablecloth trailed down almost to the floor, so I was sure that Bunty wouldn't be able to spot me. But this was no way to enjoy dinner! I was stuck between the devil and the deep blue sea. When my legs started to cramp and my stilettos began to sink into the clayey soil, I realised that Bunty was the lesser of two evils. But, as I was easing my way out, three pairs of legs suddenly came and parked themselves around the table. Luckily, the table was big enough and they weren't within touching distance of me! But how on earth was I going to emerge? And what if Bunty was around when I emerged? Nothing would be more embarrassing!

I figured that I had no choice but to stay put until the trio left, so I shifted my weight and made myself as comfortable as I could. It was a strangely mixed threesome. The guy on my left was wearing black trousers in some amazing material, with just the right shoes and socks. The lady on his right was wearing a super short red dress and black Jimmy Choos that I recognised from last month's *Vogue.* I would have had a Basic Instinct moment when she crossed her legs just then if I had not instinctively turned my head the other way round. The lady there was in a typical Karol Bagh-type *sari*—an uncomfortable fabric in shades of neon green, blue and brown, all cockled in an excess of embroidery and glitter. Her rather pudgy and hairy toes, squished into strappy sandals, looked like two iguanas cramped together inside a silver cage.

"So nice to see you here, Sudhir." Her voice was unctuous and heavy.

"Yes, Auntie*ji*, nice to see you too." Hmmm, the guy had one of those deep sonorous voices that you don't hear too often from Indian men, kinda like AB baby's.

"Silly boy, don't call me 'Auntie*ji*'! Call me Anita. I'm not *so* old!" I could almost imagine a sly simper on the Karol Bagh Auntie's face.

"So, what do you do for a living?" Ms Basic Instinct had one of those husky come-hither voices. I was dying to take a peek at these people and see if they really looked like I was picturing them in my mind.

"I'm an investment banker."

"Oh, a banker, huh? I could tell just by looking at you that you must be one of the movers and shakers . . ."

How subtle! Bitch.

"So, tell me, Sudhir, what have you been up to? Dating-*shating*, you naughty boy?" the Karol Bagh Auntie was desperate to remain in the loop.

He must have felt like he was at a Ping Pong match, trying to keep pace with the two conversations. Poor guy!

"Oh, you know, Auntie*ji*, one is so busy with work . . ."

"Not 'Auntie*ji*', Sudhir! Anita! I'm really very young, you know. I got married too early . . . why I was only seventeen when it happened. I must be your age!"

"I have always loved the world of banking. Why, at one time I myself thought I would become a banker. But what to do, Prabuddha discovered me, and that was that . . ." Ms Basic Instinct bragged snootily.

Not ready to be left behind, the Karol Bagh Auntie quickly chipped in, "Sudhir, we really must get together now that you're in town. Why don't you let me know when you're free and we can plan something?"

Clang!

A fork fell to the ground and rolled towards me. And Mr Baritone bent down to pick it up.

2

Inevitably, when he bent down, Mr Baritone looked straight at me and his eyebrows shot up to his forehead! He looked like he was about to say something, so I quickly put my finger over my lips in the universal 'Shush!' sign. Thankfully, he understood and straightened up, but not before I saw a smile on his face—a this-chick-is-crazy kind of smile. Just my luck. The one really good-looking guy I see in a long time, and it had to be like this! He was very good-looking. Thick, slightly unruly hair, big chocolaty eyes with longish eye-lashes which should have looked ridiculously effeminate but on him they actually looked darn good, a hint of stubble and full lips.

Humph!

I desultorily picked at the now-cold food on my plate, and heard the drama unfold some more. The conversational ping-pong continued between the Karol Bagh Auntie and Ms Basic Instinct, and then, as if magnetically synchronised, it happened. Karol Bagh Auntie took off her *sandal* and Ms Basic Instinct shucked off her Jimmy Choos and, at one and the same time, both their feetS made a beeline for Mr

Baritone's legs. I watched in horrified fascination as both of them began a game of footsie, unaware that that Mr Baritone had tucked away his legs, one on each side of his chair. So the next thing you knew, they were playing footsie with each other: Ms Basic Instinct locking her finely polished toes with Karol Bagh Auntie's hairy ones! I was totally enjoying this ridiculous sight when Mr Baritone pushed his chair back and said, "I'm off to get some dessert."

As their owners realised just who they'd been playing footsie with, the two feet stopped moving at once. I wish I could have seen the expressions on both of their faces! Both the women hurriedly got up and rushed off, presumably in opposite directions. I started giggling right there under the table, but when I realised that the table was probably shaking because of it, I controlled myself and began hauling myself up from under the table. Whoops! Mr Baritone was standing right there! Yeah, I really wanted a good-looking guy to see me ass-first!

"Ah . . . I was wondering when you would emerge. Tell me, do you always hide under tables at weddings?"

"It's a long story," I blushed. Yes, I blush when embarrassed and definitely when I am mortified like I was right then.

"No problem. Want to share it with me over dessert?"

I smiled at him. He really was a man after my own heart. His dinner plate was piled high with all the gooey concoctions the dessert buffet had on offer.

"Sure, but I don't think you know about the denouement, as in what chased the cats away." I parked my butt on the neon gauze-wrapped chair and reached out for a profiterole, my favourite. The hosts might not have known much about décor but they sure knew how to pick a caterer. "It turns out that your dinner dates really wanted to play footsie with you, but wound up rubbing each other the wrong way instead!"

He choked on a morsel of dessert and then threw his head back, bursting into a hearty guffaw.

"Thanks for letting me know. I thought it was my new deo which did the trick!" he shot back when he eventually stopped laughing. "I'm Sudhir, by the way. My friends call me Dhir."

"I know."

He nodded and smiled.

"So what were you really doing under the table? Are you a superspy, hiding from the evil villain who wants to get your secrets out and sell them to your enemies? An international woman of mystery?"

"Hiding all right, and from an evil villain at that, but no superspy. All I'm trying to preserve is my ring finger."

"Huh?"

"Well, there's this obnoxious guy that I've known forever and my mom's trying to hook me up with him, so I was merely dodging the bullet. Enough about me. So, going on that date with Anita Auntie?"

"Sure, as soon as I get back from the space mission. Anyhow, I'm an investment banker, as I guess you already know. What do you do?"

"I'm in advertising."

"I knew you'd be a model."

Ok, how could I not fall in lust with that line?

"Uh, no, actually I'm a writer, I write ads."

"Wow! What a wonderfully creative job."

"Well, it has its moments . . ." Dhir and I had reached for the same molten chocolate brownie at the same time, and were engaged in a tussle of forks, racing each other to the finish.

"I love to see a girl who doesn't mess with her food."

"You bet. Fight you for the *malpuas*?"

"You're on."

We had a frantic battle over every bite of the desserts Dhir had piled on his plate, and finally declared it a draw when everything had been polished off. I took off my shoes and put my aching feet up on a chair. What a life—no shoes, a dinner of desserts and a delicious man next to me.

"So tell me more about advertising. Is it as glamorous as it sounds?"

"About as glamorous as investment banking sounds, I guess. Dealing with models and film producers and the like is interesting from the outside but it's actually pretty stressful because you're dealing with creative people and fragile egos. Yet, at the end of the day, you have to make sure that the client gets exactly what he's asked for. Thankfully, we don't have to deal with the money side of things. But life at office is pretty fun. It's a casual, anything-goes culture, full of interesting characters."

Dhir smiled cutely and nodded his head. This was followed by a small, awkward pause. To break it, I asked, "Do you enjoy I-Banking?"

"Well, it has its moments. It's pretty stressful, particularly because we're dealing with huge sums of money, and if you happen to goof it up, it's unforgivable. And then we deal with CEOs of companies and so on. Therefore in terms of temperament and ego, it comes down to pretty much what you described. The office is rather formal—you know, suits and ties and hierarchy and all that."

"I know. My friend Shonali is an I-banker and she is always so hyper; it's like she has caffeine instead of blood in her veins! And practically her whole wardrobe is grey suits . . ."

"Sometimes I toy with the idea of doing something more creative . . ."

"Like what?"

"I don't know . . . my own business, maybe."

"Really? That sounds like fun!"

"It is going to be a lot of work though, and no safety net of a salary to see me through."

"What kind of business do you have in mind?"

"I'm not sure. The easiest type of business to set up nowadays would be something related to the Internet. But I won't like that too much. I'd like to do something that allows me to travel around the country and show it to other people in the way I think they should see it. I've always loved adventure sports and travel. So, some kind of specialised adventure tours, I guess . . ."

"Wow, that sounds really interesting. You should do it!"

"Well, the thought does come and bite me every six months or so, but . . ."

"But what?"

"I don't know. It's the fear of the unknown I guess. Everything's going so well right now . . . why rock the boat?"

"What if there's a better boat out there?"

The cute smile again. Sigh.

I continued, "If everyone was scared to rock the boat, to take the proverbial leap of faith, we might not have electricity, mobile phones, airplanes . . . everything new is created by someone taking that leap."

"So are you like a boat-rocker?"

"No," I had to confess sadly. "In little ways, maybe, but not in big things."

"Why not?"

I thought about that for a long moment. I had never seriously considered the question before.

"Scared. Like you. Afraid of the unknown. Afraid of getting hurt."

"But if you don't get hurt, it means you've never lived, right? You've never gone beyond what is safe, you've never seen the full potential of anything . . ." He reached out and took my right palm in his hand. The butterflies in my stomach hurriedly soared into the stratosphere and the music of the band as well as the humming of the thousands of guests receded to their rightful place—an island far, far away—so the two of us could be alone under the stars on that crisp December night.

I held my breath, wanting the moment to get frozen in time.

He moved his face closer to mine, so close I could feel his warm breath on my face. My eyes closed as I waited for the next touch . . .

"There you are! I've been running all over the place looking for you."

A douche of ice-cold water.

Abruptly jolted out of the other world, I turned around to find Bunty staring at me balefully. "Your mom is ready to go home. *Chalo*, let's go."

"I'll just come. You carry on." *Damn you.*

"No, no, she's getting impatient, and I'm not going to run all over this place again hunting for you. Come on. And why is your phone switched off?"

Ignoring him, I reluctantly turned to Dhir and said, "I'll have to go. See you around sometime . . ."

Please ask me out, make plans, something!

"Well, I'm flying back to Bombay tomorrow morning."

"Oh, you live in Bombay? . . . Well, I guess when you're next in town then?"

"Shit . . . I don't come to Delhi very often. Do you come to Bombay at all?"

"Hardly, maybe once a year . . ."

Lo-ong pause, with Bunty breathing heavily and impatiently down my back like some kind of jailer. "Look, I hate to break this up, but can we go, please?"

"Well, give me your cell number, anyway . . ." Dhir said, pushing his phone towards me.

This is the Delhi thing to do when stuck with someone you never want to meet again—exchange numbers, say goodbye, and surreptitiously delete the number a few minutes later. Is this the Mumbai thing too?

"Sure," I picked up the phone, typed my number and pushed it back towards him.

Bunty stuck an oar in again, "Look guys, scintillating as

this conversation is, I'm turning to ice standing here. Let's move, ok?"

I waved at Dhir and trudged along with Bunty dispiritedly. My glorious, romantic evening had suddenly crashed into ice-cold water and that too with an unceremonious splash. Talk about belly flops!

"Who was that guy anyway? Your Romeo? He wasn't even your type."

"What do you know about my type? He was more my type than you are."

"That's what *you* think."

Bickering, as usual, we walked on to find Mom near the entrance. Our Bunty darling dropped us home. I retired to bed, an odd sense of emptiness inside me. It was really pissing me off to think that Dhir and I may not meet again anytime soon. I was sure he had lots of girls lusting after him in Mumbai, and I was not moving there any time soon. What a complete waste of romance potential! As the cliché goes—ships that pass in the night.

No point dwelling on it. Que sera sera and all that. Oh no! I sat up in bed suddenly.

Darn, I didn't even tell him my name!

3

I woke up with a peculiar feeling in the pit of my stomach. No, not acidity. I was not that old. It was more like an elevator-drop-accompanied-by-butterflies-inside-the-stomach kind of feeling. I felt all charged up after the rendezvous with Dhir the previous night. If I were a character in a movie, Dhir would have cancelled his flight back to Bombay and waited for me, convinced I was the girl of his dreams. Then, we'd have lived happily together ever after . . .

As I jumped out of bed to get ready for the day, I started figuring out what to wear—one must be ready for opportunities to knock, right?

Should I wear my really short skirt with the shockingly expensive new leather boots (still featuring on my credit card bills!) and my dear old leather jacket with lots of dramatic make-up? Should I be the Bollywood-heroine type in my floaty lilac dress with that curly hairdo they featured in *Elle* this month? Or should I be trench-coated and wear my snazzy red beret with the red-and-black sweater I got from Bizarre?

Five changes of clothing later, I thought I was finally

dressed for whatever the day might bring. It was a grey Marks & Spencer pencil skirt, red sweater, redder lipstick and my favourite black leather jacket, teamed with the aforementioned credit-card-haunting leather boots.

Of course, Mom protested as always: "Why don't you wear a nice silk *sari, beta*? That's what we used to wear to work in winters." She was heading back to Meerut that day, and though I knew I was going to miss her, I also knew I would've gone crazy if she stayed any longer. One final satisfied look in the mirror, a big hug to Mom, and I was out of the door.

My cellphone started ringing as soon as I was out on the street. As always, it was a five-minute job to find it in my bag. God knows I have to clear my bag out one of these days, I thought and cursed myself. I suspected I even had some bus tickets from college still floating around inside somewhere.

It was Suzie. "Yep, wassup? I'm on my way," I said, without saying hello.

"Come straight to Rajendra Place. The client has been screaming about something or the other—we gotta go and sort it out."

"Oh God. Do I have to be there?"

"Of course! RSK said."

"What time?"

"Asap."

Shit! That means a costume change! This client was notoriously conservative, so we had an unofficial policy to only wear Indian clothes when we—the girls, I mean—met him. Why does this always happen on the days when I want to look and feel sexy? Somehow, I never feel sexy or even attractive in a *salwar kameez*, until and unless it is a Ritu Kumar. But given how expensive her stuff is, on my salary my wardrobe does not exactly overflow with it. It's one of my dreams that someday hers would be the only label in the *salwar-kameez* section of my room-size, walk-in closet.

Anyway, I dispiritedly trudged back and found my most conservative *salwar kameez*. Reena *Masi* had given it to me. I hated it but I had to keep it. It was beige—my least favourite colour ever—and had a horrendous violet, floral print. A warm vest inside and a *shawl* on top. Could I be any more *behenji*? And everything was totally clashing with my make-up! But who had the time?

Mom was thrilled. But I was pissed with the day already. This was supposed to be a day for something exciting to happen, and what did I get? This crappy meeting! And, for once, I had been on time when I had gotten out of the house the first time, but now, as usual I was late and had to rush to catch up. I ran towards the car, my head down, checking out the time on my phone. Crash! I collided with someone and sprawled ungracefully on the muddy strip that passes for a lawn in front of my apartment building. The contents of my bag were all over the place.

I pulled myself up into sitting position and glared at the idiot who collided into me. It was my letchy neighbour Devraj. He used to be in advertising, but is now a journalist. There was some story about him trying to grope someone someday—I didn't really know the details—but he'd been known as The Molester ever since. Labels are easy to come by and hard to live down in our business.

I started picking up the variegated contents of my bag—lipstick, near-empty wallet, eye pencil, compact, long-lasting lipstick, assorted pens with non-working refills . . .

"Is this yours?"

He picked up my emergency ST (sanitary towel)! I was tempted to disown it but realised it would be less than convincing, so I tried to look unflustered as I took it and shoved it deep down in my bag. *Yeww, I'll have to drop it in the nearest trash can!*

I muttered out a hasty "thanks" and shuffled to the car. I was furiously late by then. I was sure Suzie must have already reached the client's office. And guess what, my *salwar kameez* was all dust and was adding much beauty to my overall diva look. Aaargh!

No, my ordeal was not over. The traffic was horrendous that day and I was low on fuel. Bumper to bumper all the way, I was stuck in a jam. I turned on the radio, but the ceaseless jabber of the RJs put me off in no time. How do they do it, talk on and on like that? Honk-honk from behind. What did the moron think I was doing? Parking in traffic for the heck of it? Hello, I would move if I could! I was practically sitting on my middle finger to control myself.

Finally, we started chugging past the cause of the jam—some benighted fool was changing his tyre in the fast lane. Couldn't he at least have pulled over to the shoulder! There was plenty of space. One of these days I'm actually going to buy some old shoes just to chuck at these assholes, I thought. But at the moment, I didn't even have the time to give him one of my best dirty looks; I was too busy trying to zip through the gaps in the traffic. Suzie had already called thrice.

Finally I reached the client's office and pulled into a parking slot. As I was exiting the car, a so-called parking attendant showed up.

"Madam, you can't park here."

"Why not?"

"Madam, this is reserved."

"But it's not written anywhere! Please let me go, I'm late for my meeting!"

"Madam, you can't park here."

He was clearly a man of one idea. I ended up giving him my keys so he could park, hoping he didn't scrape the car. He looked all of thirteen and God alone knows if he could even drive.

I entered the conference room a good half an hour after Suzie. Mr Mishra, the marketing manager, gave me his toothy smile. He had the largest teeth among everyone I knew.

"So, Kajal *Meydam*, you have finally come."

"Sorry, I'm late, Mr Mishra, there was so much traffic."

I slid into place next to Suzie, trying to read her notes on the meeting so far. Suzie's handwriting was horrendous. She should have been a doctor.

A cup of overboiled tea, the colour of mud, was waiting for me with a thick layer of cream on top. I tried and choked some of it down. Mr Mishra would get upset if one didn't partake of his hospitality.

"*Heh, heh, aap to din ba din nikharti jaa rahi hain. Kis chakki ka aata khaati hain* (You're looking more gorgeous day by day, where is it coming from)?" Mr Mishra's idea of PC—polite conversation. I'd gotten used to these bizarre sallies. But Suzie had not; she was primmer by nature.

"So, Mr Mishra, back to the discussion we were having?"

"*Meydam, yeh ho kya raha hai?* We briefed you so many days back and still there is nothing . . ."

I looked at Suzie for enlightenment—which of his many briefs was he talking about?

"Mr Mishra, we have shown you so many layouts of the POP."

Oh, the design of their point of sale material—the posters and stickers they put up at stores which stock their brand. I hated the job and it caused a ruckus every year. The designs would be shown to all their sales people, and since each one of them was a closet creative director with many inane suggestions up his sleeve, nothing would get decided till the last minute. Then, like a pack of wolves, they would start baying for our blood and we would have to literally work overnight to get things done.

"Yes, but you people haven't got it right yet! The feedback has not been included. We told you our logo should be much bigger. And the colour scheme needs to be brighter, more colourful."

Their logo was bright red and yellow. How much brighter could it get?

Mr Mishra was truly an original—like many other clients, he believed he could do our job. But unlike all other clients, he actually tried to do so, with, needless to mention, disastrous results.

Every time you presented a creative to him, he listened with ill-concealed impatience until you finished. And then, "*Kyon na ispe . . . chori chhod de* (Why not cast a girl—read busty blonde—in this)?"

"*Kyon na ispe chori chhod dein*?" See! I knew it was coming. "And our product should come jooming in, no?" Mr I-can-do-this-better gave us his two favourite suggestions.

"Mishra*ji*, we will rework on the POP."

"Till when? *Hamaari truckein maal leke khadi hain* and you have not delivered the material (Our trucks are standing laden with our products but they can't go unless you give us the POP)."

I tuned out as the argument went on, periodically adding a stray comment here and there. Over the years, I'd perfected the art of appearing attentive. A skillfully placed "Yes, yes" or "Absolutely. I agree" worked wonders and left my mind free to wander.

At that time, it wandered to speculations regarding what would have happened if Dhir had been a Delhiite. Of course, he would have fallen really hard for me the previous night. We'd have gone on exciting dates, maybe even a whirlwind romantic surprise trip to Paris. Ignoring my lack-of-passport status, I pictured the super-romantic proposal he'd have made on a bended knee on a Bateau Mouche, with champagne and candlelight on the table. I was naming our second kid—a cute boy with my eyes and his voice—when Mr Mishra rudely broke in with, "Okay, so we'll see some new layouts by this evening?"

"Oh, absolutely. I agree."

What?? Oh shit, did I just agree to this stupid deadline? The CD was going to kill me!

Needless to say, the return to office was not exactly the Triumphant March it should have been. It was more like the March Slav.

Junaki, my art partner, gave me some of her best dirty looks when I explained the deadline to her.

"I had a hot date tonight," she spewed at me nastily.

"So? You can still go? We have to present this by evening, no?"

"No way am I gonna be able to come up with new layouts by evening! I must have churned out twenty-five different poster designs for that demented nut!"

"Sorry, *yaar*."

"What on earth were you thinking? Must have been off dreaming about some guy!"

This is the worst thing about working and being friends with someone for five years—they think they know you so well.

But, of course, they do!

"Well, I met this amazing guy . . ."

"Oh, no, not again."

"What do ya mean 'not again'? Have you not noticed the dating dry-spell I have been going through?"

"Yeah, two whole weeks."

Ok, I did have a tendency to date a lot, but what the heck, a girl's gotta eat!

"Well, it seems like much longer. I haven't dated a likely prospect in ages."

"So tell me, what's wrong with him? Is he too short? Too tall? Too lazy? Too ambitious? Too sweet? Too aggro?"

I confess I used to nitpick, but it was the most important decision of my life, right?

"No, too far."

"As in?"

"Lives in Bombay."

I spilled the beans about the previous evening, and as I talked about Dhir, my knees turned to mush all over again. It was such a shame that he lived so far away.

"Well, that one sorted itself out fast. Now, may I request you to turn your attention to Mr Mishra and his requirements, so that other people can have a love-life too?"

4

I hung up the phone and took a large draught of my coffee. Dad had called for his annual review.

I'd moved out of home after finishing school: first college at LSR in Delhi, then Sophia in Bombay for my post-grad in Mass Com and then back again in Delhi. I hadn't lived at home for ten years. Over the years, Dad had developed the habit of having a serious chat with me about my goals and life-plans, typically around January. I called it my annual review. Not that he expected me to turn into Madame Curie or anything; he just believes that one should be the best at whatever one does.

"*Beta*, I hope you're doing well in your career and putting in your best. You're so smart and so capable . . . you can do anything you put your mind to. But, remember, often the people who succeed in life are those who may not be very smart but those who persevere, who work hard, who have goals. It's very important to set goals for yourself. So you know what you're aiming for. You are in the prime of your life. Don't waste away these days in only having fun—they will never come back. I hope you're putting your potential to its best use." Dad has an old-fashioned, British-Empire style of talking. He also had a point.

It had been six years at the agency and I was still just a copywriter. Dating disasters came and went by, but what I really hankered after was that promotion to ACD—Associate Creative Director. It came with a number of perks: getting to supervise a couple of junior creative teams, getting a more strategic overview of the business, involvement in more pitches, getting to skip a few of those late nights too that had become overly common these days. I should face it, I just haven't been serious or committed enough. When I compared myself to the way Dad ran his career in the army or how he ran his business, or the effort that Ma put into her teaching, I felt ashamed of myself. I could do better, and what's more, it was time I did it.

I needed one good solid campaign to put my face on the map. In advertising, all it takes is the right break and suddenly you're discovered and you're a star and you find all kinds of people wooing you with fancy designations and fancier packages. Frankly, I was getting a little tired of dealing with the Mr Mishras of the world.

I decided to have a chat with our CD. He was one of the hottest in the business, workwise; otherwise he was a total d-o-g. He was built like a pit bull—kinda short and muscular. He was almost bald but you could always see some wiry body-hair poking out of his shirt. For some bizarre reason, he enjoyed wearing cowboy boots. You could hear him stomping all over the office. And did I mention a voice like a foghorn?

Whenever he talked, I always mentally pictured him with a cigar hanging out from the side of his lip.

"RKS, can I have a word?"

"Sure. What is it?"

"Well . . ."

"Ok, you had your word. If you want to have more than one, it'll have to wait."

I blinked at him, not sure if he was serious or kidding. "Har haar haar de haar haar . . ." Like Wodehouse once said, his laugh was like the sea crashing over some seriously broken rocks. "Just kidding, ok! Come on in. What's on your mind?"

"I just . . . just . . ." For a copywriter, I was not too great with words, especially in a serious work-type situation.

"Yes, spit it out."

"I've been thinking . . ."

"That's new." Yeah, advertising really isn't for sensitive, poetic-type souls. You get stomped on all the time in our world.

"I want something more challenging than what I've been doing so far. Not that I don't love doing POP or leaflets or even those teeny little newspaper ads for ten percent discounts, but, you know, I want to work on a really big campaign now."

"Oh, you do, huh?"

"Yes, I do. I want to do something more interesting, something exciting . . ."

"What's the matter? Love-life letting you down?"

Ok, my love-life was somewhat of a joke in the office, what with the revolving door and all, but it had nothing to do with my job!

"Ha, ha, very funny. Seriously, RKS, I feel like I'm in a

rut doing the same old things over and over again. The only TV ads I've made are for sales promos. Buy one, get one free. How creative can you get with that! Look, I'm six years old in the ad business. I should move to the next level, no?"

"Are you seriously serious about this?"

"Yes. I've always been serious about work. You know that."

"Right. Like the time you left in the middle of that huge tourism pitch because you had a date? Or the other time when we had to crack a lighting campaign and you had to go to a wedding?"

I knew my early sins had been pretty bad, but come on, that was way in the past. I had grown up since then.

"RKS, that's a low blow. That was over six months ago. I've changed now."

"Right."

"No, really! Would I have come up to have this conversation with you last year?"

"No, I guess not. Look, you're a crackling writer but what you've been missing is application. I've been watching you for some time now. The problem is you just don't give it your best shot, because so often your mediocre shot is enough. If anyone else with less talent than you had done that, they'd be out on their ear by now. The only reason you've been kept on, time after time, is because you have the spark!" RKS turned all serious. "If you really want to go places, if you want to be the success you can be, you must focus. Not only put your brain into stuff but also your heart and soul. You have the talent, now put in the perspiration."

The intensity in his voice got me. "I will." I said the words like a pledge, just that my right arm wasn't outstretched. If RKS thought I had talent, then I was going to do whatever it took to get there. Right then, I made a commitment to myself: "This will be my make-or-break year, the year in which I will put my career first and earn that promotion. Or else!" If it didn't, I'd . . . go home to Meerut and ask Ma to marry me off to Bunty! (No, just kidding, but I vowed that come what may that year, I was not going to let anything sidetrack me from that promotion.)

"All right then." RKS's voice, as if embarrassed by the serious tone, turned a little gruff. "Get back to work. The next time something big blows along, I'll consider you."

5

"Hey, you'll never guess what's happening. They're relaunching the Silver!" Anuj burst into the cabin.

"Who's going to relaunch what?"

"The Xiada account, silly. They're going to relaunch the Silver and we're invited for the pitch." Anuj said and hurried out to tell others the news.

Anuj was the account executive (meaning junior gopher) on the Xiada account, India's biggest automobile company.

"Don't wet your pants in the excitement," I called after him. He had a tendency to get hyper about everything. I went back to my re-draft of the script. Papercups and Boards, one of our clients, was planning some new venture and I had been handed the job of writing the script for the audio-visual (AV) film. Normally, I would have sneered at it and made a royal pain of myself to the servicing team, but my chat with RKS (and Dad) was still vivid in my mind, so I had decided to knuckle down, give it my all, keep a stiff upper lip and all other boy-scout-type clichés.

The problem with writing scripts for AV films is that

very often the client wants to pay only about a quarter of a pittance to get it made. So you're stuck with a stealomatic—wherein you scotch tape bits and pieces from other ads and movies and tie everything together with a script. Sometimes, of course, these do turn out very well, but it's not quite the same as shooting a film out on location, you know. Anyway, my nose was getting all blunt from the grindstone when what Anuj had said hit me.

"Ok, I can almost see the lightbulb glowing over your head. What crazy idea have you come up with now?" Junaki asked me.

"Why does it have to be crazy?"

"Because it's your idea."

"Oh, come on, that's hardly fair! Anyway, this is a great one. Let's tell RKS we want to work on the Silver account."

"Hey, that's not half as bad! I've never done a car campaign before."

We marched off to RKS's office and came back triumphant. We were officially on the pitch team. Of course, so were half a dozen other creative teams. The account was very big. The Silver had been one of India's biggest car launches at its time. But a whole host of other cars had come along since then and its lustre had dimmed a little. The client now wanted to re-launch it as a zingy sports car, but with no changes to the way the car looked. It was going to look the same as it had done five years ago when it had first been launched.

"That's like Waheeda Rehman wanting to come back to ingénue roles with no Botox!" I had complained.

"We'll be sure to convey your opinion to the client!" RKS

had sneered. "The research agency is presenting their findings tomorrow afternoon at the client's office. Be there."

6

Nothing is more soul-deadening than a research agency presentation. By the time they get through the two-hundred-thousand-nine-hundred-and-fifty-third piece of data on the five-hundred-and-fortieth slide of the presentation, you just wish you were in an active little profession like dish-washing.

We staggered weakly out of the room four hours later, our knees sagging. "I didn't understand one word of what they said. Did you? Why do they have to drone on and on? It's like they take boring pills before they start talking!" I complained to Junaki.

"Well, essentially what we were saying in about five hundred Powerpoint slides was that people think the Silver is a great drive, but they forget it when it comes to making their list of cars to choose from. Does that help?"

I turned around to see this hip guy with a rockstar hairstyle—cut really close to the scalp—and a soul patch. I love soul patches, especially since *Dil Chahta Hai*. "Who are you?"

"Head bore. Otherwise known as Rocky. From the research agency."

I turned bright red. Really, can I ever not make a fool of myself around a cute guy?

"Sorry about that."

"Yeah, well, you really hurt me. Ouch. You're going to have to pay me back."

"Oh?"

"Yes, with a coffee at the Barista right here."

"Well, I got things to do and places to be, so see you later," Junaki trilled and took off, wiggling her fingers at me. That girl was born tactful.

"So . . . it really took you guys five hundred Powerpoint slides to say that?" I asked, sipping my frothy cappuccino.

"Well, what can I say? You gotta make people believe you're worth the money, right?"

"Oh, so all that was for the client's benefit?"

"Yes, and for the suits. They really get turned on by all the numbers. So, are you a suit or . . .?"

I was almost insulted. He thought I was in servicing! "Nope, copywriter. What exactly do you do at your research agency?"

"Like I said, I show clients how their money was spent by making up boring presentations. I also kick butt around the office. But apart from that, I'm a real fun guy."

"How can I take your word for that? That too, with just five words—no Powerpoint, no three-hundred-something slides."

"Well, hang out with me and you'll find out. I think my boring pill is about to wear off!"

We wound up dancing on the tables at a lounge bar later that night, so I guess he was right.

"How do you always get these hot men?" Junaki whined the next day.

"I guess the talent of embarrassing myself helps. By the way, we better get down to work, if we don't wanna embarrass ourselves in front of RKS."

As usual the campaign brief from the suits was about as much help as a colander for serving soup. We'd have to do the grunt work ourselves. I did get a copy of the research presentation—all 14 MB of it—but it was daunting to even think about opening it.

While Junaki frantically googled to find more information about the car, I looked through the black book to strike out whatever had been done before from our list of ideas. There was no way I wanted anyone to even hint that our stuff was a copy of some international campaign.

The thing that got to me was that car ads are so compulsively similar. They all show the same terrific shots of a car plunging through the mud, if it is an SUV, or driving past pretty miles of countryside, all lit up like a supermodel, if it is a sedan. There is nothing about what is under the hood—the heart of the car, its personality.

I had to ask Rocky to help us decipher some of the car info—all those RPMs and so on—since neither J nor I had a mechanical turn of mind. There was no way on earth that I was going to allow the other creative groups—mostly all-male—to make fun of our ignorance.

This time, when the internal presentation deadline came around, Junaki and I were all prepared.

"So, who goes first?"

The internal review is like a game of Russian roulette. You never know when your number is up.

"Ok, so no one has come up with any ideas?"

We all avoided eye-contact with RKS. Rumour had it that he was in a foul mood that day and obviously no one was up for hara-kiri.

"Well, then. Kajal, you begged to be a part of this pitch. What have you come up with?"

Normally, I talk a blue streak, but when presenting my creative ideas before others, I have to forcibly prevent myself from wincing. It's like setting a newborn baby down on the road in rush-hour traffic and stepping back to see what happens.

"Er . . . well . . . er . . .," I could feel my cheeks turning crimson courtesy the sudden spotlight. I think I was literally giving off heat. I looked desperately at Junaki, SMS-ing her with my eyes to take over. She was even worse than me at presenting.

"You see," she began in a high-pitched voice, "the best thing about the Silver is its great drive-ability." On realising that she was practically squeaking, she brought her voice down to a deadpan. "If the drive-feel is the most unique thing about it, we should demonstrate it, no? So, we thought about a campaign that shows how people feel when they're driving it. Walter Mitty types."

"What Hello Kitty type?" one of the suits sniggered.

"Walter Mitty, ya! Like that old serial, Mungeri Lal something, with that Raghubir Yadav chap?"

"Oh, that's sexy, that'll sell a sports car. Great brand ambassador!"

"No, not him in person! That thing . . ."

I jumped in; I had to try and rescue this disaster in the making. "*Mungerilal ke Haseen Sapne.* Well, basically daydreaming. You know how people like to imagine themselves as living a different life or being someone else, someone rich or famous or really cool. That's what the drive-feel of this car does. It transports them to their ideal world . . ."

"What's the campaign, girls?"

I suddenly couldn't bring myself to read it, so I silently handed out our layouts. Layouts are mock-ups of ads for magazines or newspapers, where you put a representative picture and the copy. Junaki and I had come up with this idea of superimposing haikus on a series of visuals that showed what the guy was imagining. Haikus are hard work because each of their three lines has to have a set number of syllables, so each word has to be just the right fit. Composing a haiku is like finding the perfect setting for a precious stone. I have always loved this exacting and precise form of poetry but, somehow, I feel poetry is even more difficult to show to someone than prose. It is intensely more personal after all. Our layouts were stunning—like Japanese paintings. I had slaved night after night on the haikus, something that had pissed off Rocky to no end because I'd had to cancel our plans every evening for them. Junaki had kept me company all through this, dreaming up the visuals et al. There was a long pause as the ads were passed around the table.

"Har har de haar haar!"

"Good joke, guys, where's the real campaign?"

"What are you, kidding? This is supposed to be targeting the Delhi dudes?"

"If you want to start doing manga, do it on your own time, babes. Where's the campaign?"

I was frozen in my place, the blush receding from my face and an icy-cold feeling enveloping my bones, as if I'd been dropped head first into the Arctic Ocean. I looked over at Junaki, stricken, and saw that her face looked pale and pinched, perhaps like mine. I opened my mouth to defend our work, but no words came out. I wanted to reach out and gather my poems and the lovely layouts and hold them close to me and run out of the room to never come back . . .

As always, what we did in reality was very different: we slowly sat down with strained smiles while the roulette carried on to find other targets. My mind was whirling from both lack of sleep and disgraceful humiliation. This was supposed to have been my big break, our big break—Junaki's and mine—though she cared much less than me about promotions and ambitions and all that scary stuff. But, it had turned out to be a fiasco, and I didn't know whom or what to blame.

Later, RKS called us into his room.

"So, what happened?" he asked gruffly. "I thought you were going to work really hard on this, without goofing up?"

Embarrassingly, tears started leaking out of my eyes, even as I tried my best to control them. "But . . . but . . . we did work hard. We were the only team who even understood the problem with the car. We worked all night the whole week putting this together . . ."

Junaki nodded, "It's true, we haven't seen daylight in the past week; we've been so busy working on this."

"No dates for a whole week? You really have been working then!" RKS gave me a thump on the back so hard that I almost fell down. He had the strength of a gorilla. "Well, back to the drawing board. It's not the end of the world. You have a great idea there—the ideal world, Walter Mitty and all. Yes, I studied English Lit in college too! But you have to bring it down to earth; look at the real consumer here. You're not writing for the Booker Prize, but for the Abbies—the Bombay Ad Club Awards. And for the sales the campaign will generate. Talk to the real target audience, real people like your neighbours and relatives, and not other ad types. And then think about how you'll make this proposition work for them."

I sat up, struck by this. "You're right. Of course, we've been imagining some completely different kind of consumer."

"Of course, I'm right. I'm the boss, remember?" RKS's voice was back to normal and booming. "Now get out of here. I want to see the new campaign by Friday. That's your last chance for this pitch."

7

J and I decided to take a break from the hectic campaign and take the evening off. We needed some time apart. Rocky was stuck at work, so I started back home. I was finally in a decent mood because at the end of the day RKS had said that the basic idea was fine. It was the execution that needed tweaking. I was picturing the evening ahead: a nice long soak in the tub with a good book and a glass of wine, followed by a Domino's, when the car started emitting funny CLONK-CLANGing sounds.

I looked at the fuel gauge, which is pretty much the only thing I know about cars. Nope, there was enough fuel. What could it be? I was hoping the problem wouldn't be anything serious enough to warrant a visit to the garage when the car completely died. Right in the middle of traffic! I tried to restart it, but it was a no go. The other cars made their way past, casting dirty looks at me. I heard a few derisive shouts of 'lady driver!' also. How nice!

I got out and tried to push the car to the shoulder of the road, but with no luck. Luckily, a couple of hulking guys loitering by the roadside rushed up to me. "*Medam, hum kar denge* (We'll do it for you)."

I felt annoyingly damsel-in-distress-like, watching the two push my car to the side of the road with what seemed like a flick of their fingers. I was wondering how much to tip them when they turned towards me, dusting their hands off, "*Meddum, aur kuch kar sakte hain aapke liye* (Can we do anything else for you)?"

"*Nahin*, thank you, *dhanyavaad*." I proffered two hundred rupees. They didn't take it.

"*Kya, meddum, paise de rahi hain . . . Chaliye aapko ghar chhod dein (Ma'am we don't need the money . . . Let us drop you home).*"

They said it in a perfectly harmless manner, but something about their tone made my mind start replaying Hindi movie scenes featuring Prem Chopra, Shakti Kapoor and the like.

Struggling to keep fear out of my voice and backing away, I said, "*Nahin, nahin*, it's ok, *main apne aap chali jaoongi* (No, it's ok, I will manage on my own)."

"*Meddum, humne kaha na, paise ki zaroorat nahin hai. Aapko ghar chhod dete hain, koi* problem *nahin . . . lagta hai baarish aane wali hai* (Ma'am, we told you, you don't need to pay. Let us drop you home. It's ok . . . Seems it's going to rain)."

They seemed to loom up on me. I glanced around frantically but could only see a swarm of cars and trucks, too busy maneuvering against each other at rush hour to notice what was happening at the roadside. I lost my head and took off down the highway, pursued by the honks and beeps of a million cars and far away shouts of '*Meddum*'! Several minutes later, with a stitch in my side, I finally ground to a halt and looked around, panting. Those guys had given up the chase, thankfully. As I stood there, hoping to spot a cycle rickshaw, I felt a big drop of water on my face. I looked up at the sky only to realise that the grey clouds had decided their time had come!

In Gurgaon, it never just rains, it pours and that's exactly what happened then. Minutes later, I was soaked right down to my undies. There was no way I could even hope to get a cycle rickshaw or taxi in weather like that. I had to walk all the way home! And it had to be in my new suede shoes on a sodden, god-forsaken day like that! ☹

The road was full of slush and mud and the walk home never-ending. Just putting one foot in front of the other was a monumental effort. I'd already had a cold for a couple of days. By the time I reached the colony gates, I was swaying on my feet. I still made it up to the elevators to lift one hand to press the down button . . . and that's the last thing I remember doing . . .

When I came to, I was so tightly ensconced in a snug bunch of quilts that I couldn't even move my arms. The room was dimly lit; I spotted bamboo chick blinds on the window . . . and then I drifted off to sleep again. Later, I had a vague memory of someone patting my head and smoothing my hair back, feeding me something cool at one point and forcing me to swallow some tablets at another.

After another long while, I woke up, feeling much better. I looked around and found that I was alone in a room I didn't recognise. It was nice though, with earthy, beige-toned walls, gleaming white paintwork on the doors, bamboo chicks and lamps and some nice black-and-white prints on the walls. Nothing too ethnic or too international. Nice and homey. A low bookshelf full of books lined one wall. If I could have extricated myself from my cocoon of quilts, I'd have liked to walk over and take a look at the books. I feel you can tell so much about a person from the books they have and, of course, by whether they have a bookshelf at all or not. I wondered where on earth I was—the layout of the room was familiar, but I had never been in this room before. I heard someone bustling about outside the room and called out, "Um . . . hello?"

You'll never guess who walked into the room.

Devraj— Debu! The Molester! You remember the creep who picked up my sanitary towel? That's who!

As casually as if he were a buddy, he said, "Oh, hi, you're finally up . . ."

"What the HELL are *you* doing in here?" It suddenly dawned on me exactly where I was. I was instantly horrified, shocked and terrified by the thought of whatever that had been done to me in my unconscious state. I wiggled my limbs and realised I was in a nightie of some kind, all bunched up around my hips. There could only be one person who had undressed me. To think I'd managed to get away from those lecherous dogs on the road only to get caught by this awful bastard!

"What have you been doing to me, you creep! How could you do this to me, you monster?" I started crying and shouting at the same time. I was feeling completely at his mercy, being so tightly tucked into that darned bundle of quilts.

"Listen, calm down, let me . . ."

"Let you WHAT, you molester? How dare you bring me here?" I thrashed about violently, trying to get out of the hideous bed. "Get out. GET OUT!"

The creep's face acquired an angry look. I was trying to tell myself to try and pacify him lest he do something worse to me when he turned and walked out of the room. As soon as I heard a distant door slam somewhere, I practically overturned the bed, fighting my way out of the quilts. I looked around the room and spotted my clothes and bag in a corner. My suede shoes lay pathetically awry in a corner, like forlorn puppies. I picked up my bag and clothes and was getting ready to make a run for it before the monster reappeared when I heard the front door open again. I held my breath and then—oh, blessed event—I heard Mrs Mohammed, of the flat above mine. "Kajal, *beta* . . ."

I ran and clung to her like a barnacle. We had never exactly been bosom buddies—she disapproving of my late-nights lifestyle, and me disapproving of her disapprovals—but at that minute, she was surrounded by a chorus of angels.

"Thank God you've come, Auntie! Please, help me get out of here before that creep comes back!"

"What creep?"

"That . . . that . . . Devraj. He . . . I was ill . . . and I think he . . . he must have brought me here when I was unconscious and . . ."

"Yes, he did," she said calmly.

I blinked and stared at her. Was she in league with him?

"You apparently collapsed right outside the lift downstairs.

He was going out and almost stepped on you. He brought you up here and then called me to look after you. He has been very sweet, that boy. Called a doctor and made her come here and take a look at you."

"Oh . . ." my voice trailed away. "I do remember someone sponging my head and giving me medicine . . ."

"That was me. The poor boy slept out in the drawing room, in case you needed a doctor or in case you called in the night or something. I put you in my nightie."

I looked down at myself. I was clad in a thick, hideously brown nightie which would have sent even the most despo guy screaming in the other direction.

"But why are you out of bed, *beta*? And what was all that shouting about? I thought you had become delirious or something. I had just gone back home for a bath, when I heard all these noises."

OH!!! Remember in *Alice in Wonderland*, when she drinks that shrinking potion? Somebody must have slipped me some right that minute for I suddenly felt smaller than the smallest dung beetle that ever lived.

"Come on, get back into bed, before you get worse."

"Auntie, I'd prefer going home."

"Okay. I'll stay with you today in case you need any help. Shall I?"

"Thanks so much, Auntie."

8

We made our way up one floor to my flat, which was exactly over Devraj's flat. I have to say, the effort of walking slowly to the lift and walking from the lift to my front door was enough to tire me out.

Auntie unlocked my door and helped me inside. I promptly collapsed on the *divan*. But then I sat up again and asked, "How come Devraj didn't bring me to my flat?"

"He didn't have the key. It wasn't in your purse either. I looked for it, because he said it wouldn't be polite for him to look. He's a sweet boy. Who finds boys like him in a big city nowadays?"

"So how come you have it now?" I sank back down on the *divan*.

"I think he found it in your car the day before. He brought it and gave it to me. But I said you were too ill to be moved, so we just took care of you in his flat only till you woke up today."

I sprang up again at the mention of my car. "Auntie, my car! I left it on the road, thinking I'd call for help once I got back. God knows what's happened to it by now!"

"No, no, don't worry, and lie down! Devraj got your car towed to a service center.

"*Accha*, now you need rest. Do you want some good *adrak chai*?" She puttered around, fluffing pillows and tucking me into the *divan*, chattering on about her family.

Oh God, as if I needed any more reasons to grovel in front of Devraj, I thought to myself. I was just getting ready to lie down when I heard a far-off telephone bell ring, and suddenly remembered I hadn't checked my messages. Heavens! What day was it? We had to come up with a new campaign by Friday. Hmm, let's see, the Hara-kiri Day had been Monday . . .

"Auntie, what day is today?" I ruthlessly interrupted her.

"What . . . why? It's Thursday."

"Oh, no!" I exclaimed loudly, swinging my legs off the *divan* onto the floor. "I better get ready and get to work."

"Are you crazy? You have barely recovered from your fever! It was really very high."

"Yes, Auntie, but I have something absolutely critical that needs to be done by tomorrow."

"What? You're not a nuclear scientist *na* that Pokhran will get delayed if you rest at home for one more day? Back to bed you go!" I shied like a horse, but she was pretty cunning. "Back to bed, or I call your parents and tell them how ill you've been and how you're insisting on going back to work."

I sulkily got back onto the *divan* and glared at her, though I was secretly kind of grateful, because that brief moment out of bed had made me tremble like a jelly. I didn't want my folks getting wind of this fever or whatever it was. My parents were cool enough as a rule, but they were perennially paranoid about my health. I had once gone out of town for a school camp or something and had fallen so seriously ill that it had been touch-and-go for a while. Ever since, if I'm ever ill and they're not by my bedside, they worry themselves sick, or worse, they land up and stay for months with me. Not that I didn't love them to bits, but whenever both Mom and Dad would be there to see me, they would start acting all over-protective. *Are you warm enough? Are you sure you should be wearing that? Why are you working so late? Should you be eating that? Shouldn't you be exercising more?* And so on and so forth till I would be ready to burst. Having flown the coop years ago, it was much harder for me to fly back in. It is when I visit them, but when they come to visit me, they cramp my style. And then I feel guilty about it, but never guilty enough to desire a visitation on my head.

"Fine, then may I at least have my cell phone?"

"Okay, but remember not to overwork. You people never understand the value of rest."

I quickly pulled out my phone, plugged it in to charge and checked my calls. I had, like, twenty-one missed calls from Junaki.

"Hey."

"Don't hey me! Where the fuck have you been? The campaign's due tomorrow and you've been playing hide-and-seek. RKS has been asking all over for you and I've had to cover like crazy. Why didn't you answer your phone?" I held the phone a good foot away from my ear and waited patiently until she had screeched herself out.

"Didn't it occur to you, Miss Junaki, that since I wasn't

answering the phone or coming to office, I could have been kidnapped or something?"

"Haha. Good one. Anyone who kidnaps you would pay to give you back. But this is one of your worst bunks! Whatever happened to the copywriter-of-the-year dreams, ACD and all that?"

"For your information, I happen to have been extremely ill and, in fact, completely unconscious for the past two days," I informed her witheringly.

"What shit, really?"

"Yes, really. If you think I'd be so irresponsible as to go off and leave a huge campaign in the lurch . . ."

"I just thought you'd gone off somewhere with Rocky for a rock-fest, if you know what I mean."

"Uhh, no way, Rocky and I aren't *that* involved yet. Anyway, this is no time to be discussing my love-life or other extraneous matters. Listen, I really have been horrendously ill and can't come to the office. Can you come here so we can work from here? And worm that laptop out from the servicing department—the one with the Internet access card—so we can do the layouts sitting right here. Okay?"

"But what'll I tell RKS?"

"I dunno . . . the truth? Or, wait. Just sneak out of office if you can and tell someone you're going to Barista with me or something. I don't want him to know I've been out of action right before a big pitch. Let's do the campaign and show him, then we'll tell him. It'll sound better, given my track record."

"Okay. See ya."

I knew there was a huge, giant apology that needed to

happen, but right then, I was too sick to get out of bed. Not to mention too horrified. Till Junaki arrived, I kept replaying the scene with Devraj over and over in my mind. Nope. I hadn't left myself even an inch of wiggle-room. I would have to eat mud, heck, eat crow, and basically grovel all over the guy's feet. I couldn't believe I had been such a complete jack-ass. It made me almost break out in hives every time I thought about it.

Luckily, Junaki arrived with all the goss from office: about how so far none of the other teams seemed to have cracked anything and about who'd just broken up with whom. The review meeting was set for the next morning, 11 a.m., so we really had no time at all if we wanted the office printer—which had an evil penchant of going bust right before a deadline—to print out any of our layouts.

"Ok, so the basic proposition of dream world is fine. It's how we put it across that needs to be decided. Think, think, how to do it?"

"Why don't we put little thought-blurbs?"

"Any other clichés you have up your sleeve?"

We hadn't cracked anything by evening, and our bean-feast had descended to frank bickering when Mrs Muhammed poked her head back in. "Have you girls eaten dinner?"

"No, Auntie, we'll order something later, thanks," I told her.

"Nonsense. Food is ready. I'll just bring both of you a hot meal. You look like as if a strong breeze will knock you down, both of you. Girls in our days used to be nice and curvy, not so thin."

"Auntie, we're really busy with work. I mean, thanks so

much for the offer, I really appreciate it. Maybe I can eat over at your house another time? But right now . . ."

"Right now nothing. You girls have been working so hard all day. Surely you can take the time out for a good, hot, home-cooked meal? The brain also needs rest. And you'll be able to think better with some good food inside you. Come on, I've made some lovely *maa ki daal* and *bhindi*. There's *gajar ka halwa* too."

The mention of the actual dishes wiped away all our resistance. "Thanks so much, Auntie. That sounds wonderful. We'll just come."

"No, no, I don't want you stirring out of bed. Doubtless, you'll pull another fainting fit if that happens, and I can't even lift you up. I'll bring your food right here."

"And yours, Auntie? Have you eaten?"

"No, I'll eat at home," she protested, but I knew she must be lonely. Her kids were grown up and lived by themselves now and she'd been widowed for about four years.

"No, no, Auntie, please do join us. I won't eat if you don't."

"Naughty girl," she said, but with a twinkle in her eyes, and flounced out, with Junaki in her wake to help her get the food.

9

Auntie had severely understated the menu, both in terms of quality and quantity. The dishes smelled heavenly as they were brought in. We quickly sat down on the bed, our plates heaped with food. I idly flicked the TV on to an old Hindi movie channel. I love watching oldies when I'm ill at home—they're so comforting: everyone is nice in them, except the villain, and you know he pays for his villainy in the climax. *Awara* was on and we all started watching it. I was fascinated despite myself. Raj Kapoor is at his least Chaplin-esque self and his proud lover moments had me melting into a puddle. For no reason at all, Dhir's face popped into my head. I was impressed I still remembered his name, and smiled.

"*Ghar aaya mera pardesi . . .*" Mrs Muhammed sang out loud and sighed. "I always loved the dream sequences in the old movies: the clouds came in, the music changed and everything became so romantic in a heartbeat . . ." she reminisced, while we cleaned our plates of the last bits of the delicious *halwa*. "*Aisa lagta tha* anything is possible."

"Who was your favourite hero?" I asked her, teasing.

She giggled like a schoolgirl, instead of the over-60 Grandma that she was, and said, "Dharmendra. My God, he was so handsome. I used to feel faint if I even saw a poster of his. I lived in Bombay before marriage, in Juhu, and all these film stars could be seen there from time to time, driving their fancy, imported cars. I used to dream of bumping into Dharmendra in his huge Cadillac with the big fins. Gul Sahab (that's what she called her husband) also bought a Cadillac, you know, just after we got engaged. He would drive down from Poona to visit me, and we would go for long drives. Of course, I could never be alone with him, so one of my brothers or sisters, or sometimes an aunt, would come along. I was too shy to talk to him at that time, so I just used to enjoy the drive and stare at him. He was so handsome, and after he bought the Cadillac, I thought he was just like Dharmendra . . ."

I stared at her, doubtfully. I had seen a picture of the late Mr Muhammed in her flat once. To compare that bald, stout man wearing his bushy moustache with a suit that had such loud checks that you could hear them if you stood too near the photo frame, with Dharmendra, was . . . whatever . . .

After dinner, Mrs Muhammed left us, with an admonition not to be up too late. We nodded without the slightest intention of obeying her and settled back to bickering about the campaign. All of a sudden, inspiration struck me. "I've got it!" I shrieked, jumping off the *divan* in my excitement.

"What? What?"

"Mrs Muhammed and Dharmendra!"

Junaki gave me one incredulous look and then instantly got what I wanted to say. Immediately, the two of us were off on a creative roller coaster, each of us describing a different piece of the work, but each of us getting what the other was saying. We were all flushed with the triumph of the brainwave. "Thank God for Mrs Muhammed," Junaki cried, as she quickly created a series of images on the laptop. "And thank God you fell ill. Otherwise we'd never have chatted with her."

We stayed up till the wee hours of the morning; we were both too het up and too busy to sleep. J showered at my place, borrowed a skirt and top from me, and we cabbed down to work.

RKS was out for a meeting and was to come in for the review only at eleven, so I didn't even get a chance to tell him I'd been sick.

For once, we all gathered around the conference table sharply on time, exchanging worried glances. I took a deep sip of my over-sweet machine coffee to get some energy back. I was worn out from the illness and the all-night work.

"So, Miss Kajal has finally decided to grace the office again?" RKS derisively bellowed the moment he walked into the room. "What, did you have a bad manicure and it was too much for your heart? Or some rock concert you just had to attend?"

Uh oh! He was really pissed about my absence. Explanations sure weren't going to work while he was in this mood. And I really hadn't done myself any favours in the past, had I?

"Err . . . um . . ."

"So since you've enjoyed a nice break, I assume you have a Cannes-winning campaign idea. Go ahead, shoot."

RKS slouched in his chair at the head of the table and put

his feet up on the chair next to his, looking expectantly at me like a lion eyeing slaves in the Colosseum.

I gulped and hoped the campaign we'd come up with would pass muster.

"We thought we could do a series of dream sequences, like in the old Hindi films, you know—the car starts in a city somewhere . . . ordinary guy driving . . . and as he drives, music starts playing and the background becomes something beautiful or rich . . . then a pretty girl is sitting next to him . . ."

"Hmm . . ." Was I imagining it or was RKS sitting up straighter as I spoke? "Go on . . ."

"The film opens with an ordinary-looking guy. He comes out of his house and gets into his car. Nice beauty shot of the car, gleaming and all that. You can see the road, which is pot-holed; there is a vegetable seller with a cart; the road looks dusty and narrow and the houses are ordinary. The music is very rustic and jingle-jangly; cars are honking in the background. The minute he lets out the clutch and changes gears, the entire scenery around dissolves and morphs into a scene from Switzerland or something—the road is smooth and lined with trees; you can see a mountain or the sea in the distance; the wind is whooshing through his hair; the music becomes romantic but peppy; he drives past poppy fields and sees a beautiful woman by the side of the road, asking him for a lift. He screeches to a halt and smiles at her. She smiles back. But as he gets out of the car to open the door for her, the scenery around him dissolves right back to the middle of ordinary city traffic: cars are honking, the sun is shining. He shakes his head and takes another look at the girl. Thankfully, she's still beautiful. He gets back into the car next to her and as he lets in the clutch, the romantic music starts again. Cut to logo, and the line: 'It's a beautiful life in the Silver lane'.

"We thought we could build a whole series around it—you know, in the next film we could have them fighting in the beginning. Then the minute they get into the car, they are singing a song and driving through Switzerland . . ."

There was silence around the table for a minute as I wound down. Junaki and I shared a quick look at each other, full of apprehension. Had we got it wrong again?

"Good. Good work. Needs a little tightening. The line is too long. Let's make it shorter. What about the press campaign?"

"We're still working on that. But it's basically the same concept: we're thinking of showing the guy driving his car—the city road shot—but outside the windshield is the scenic picture."

"That sounds complicated. Work it out and show it to me this afternoon. Now, who's going next?"

TS Eliot was so right about the world ending with a whimper and not a bang. I had expected fireworks, maybe a clap on the back, or at least for everyone to burst into cheers, saying, "We did it!" But nothing happened. I guess that's the difference between sitcoms and real life.

Anyway, Junaki and I were still pleased with ourselves and were looking forward to the presentation before the client. In the meantime, however, I had a gigantic humble pie to eat, and I wasn't even sure if I was hungry.

10

I wasn't sure exactly how I'd go about it and Junaki was no help either. First she thought the whole thing was hilarious—and I mean fall-off-your-chair hilarious. "The idea of you—YOU—coming across like a Victorian maiden aunt is too funny!" she chortled. "And only you could have made a booboo this big."

"Look, I didn't do it on purpose. I'd been ill and woke up in a nightie to find this guy in the room. This, right after I had to flee down the highway to get away from some perverts. And he does have a bad rep, you know."

"Well, what are you going to do?"

"Move!"

"No, really. How exactly are you going to get over this one?"

"I don't know. Do you think if I ignore it long enough, it'll go away?"

"Uh . . . that would be no. I know you; you'll remain consumed with guilt until you've sorted it out. So you might as well get it over with."

"I guess so. Do you think flowers will help?"

"Sure. I'll put them on your grave."

"You're so comforting!"

It had been a long and exhausting day, made worse by the thought of that apology. I wasn't looking forward to the weekend as I reached home. Mrs Muhammed poked her head in to ask if I wanted dinner but I talked her out of it. I just wanted to lounge by myself. I was hungry though and my mind begun to profusely salivate at the thought of a pizza. A call to Domino's made me feel a little better. I shucked my shoes and poured myself a glass of Merlot. The Doors kicked off on my iPod and I sank back into my favourite, comfy chair—threadbare-but-loved-to-death—closed my eyes and gave myself up to the music.

The drumbeats got awfully loud all of a sudden and then I heard someone shouting too. What's that about? I thought fuzzily and opened my eyes wide with an effort. The drumbeats were still pounding, but they were weirdly overlaid on Nusrat's Night Song. Curiouser and curiouser, I thought, and shook my head to clear it. The drumming was still on, with heavy thuds in the middle.

I finally got it—someone was banging on the front door. Oh, it must be the pizza guy, I thought, and opened the door. Devraj and Mrs Muhammed crashed through as soon as I opened the door, both of them looking worried. Devraj also looked mad as hell.

"What's wrong with you, *beta*?" Mrs Muhammed cried. "Are you all right?"

"Sure," I said, yawning. "I'm fine, why?"

"Some fellow with a pizza was here and he said he rang the

bell many times but no one answered. I heard him ringing the bell so I stepped out and paid for it. Then I came to give it to you and rang the bell but you didn't answer. Since I knew you were at home, I got very worried. I thought you had fallen ill again or something, so I went and got Devraj. We have both been banging on your door for hours."

"Oh . . . oh . . . so sorry, Auntie. I must have fallen asleep; I never heard anything."

"I told you she was trouble. I told you there was nothing wrong with her!" Devraj said angrily.

"*Accha baba*, but you were also worried *na*?" said Mrs Muhammed to Devraj. "This crazy fellow was trying to break down the door just now," she said to me defensively.

"I just wanted to make sure there was no fire or anything," Devraj said in a surly tone and turned to leave.

"Won't you stay for pizza?" I cracked the box open.

Mrs Muhammed said, "I've already had dinner. You two carry on. Now that I know you are all right, I can rest at ease," and left, leaving a conversational black hole the size of a supernova behind her.

Devraj turned to go without a word. I reflexively said, "Please . . . can you stay for pizza?"

A chilly "No, thank you!" ensued from him.

I went up to him and put my hand on his arm. "Please stay. I really, really, really need to apologise to you for what I said yesterday. I was totally out of line. I'd do anything to take the words back. I'm so sorry I can't even begin to explain."

After a long, long moment, I saw his shoulders relax. I hadn't even realised until then how stiff with tension he was. "It's ok," he mumbled and tried to walk out of the apartment.

"I really did mean the pizza-offer. I don't want to chew through the cardboard all by myself. Please stay for dinner?" I begged.

At last he turned around. "Ok."

The pizza had turned cold and stiff, as I'd predicted. The wine helped us choke it down. We talked about all kinds of stuff—music, movies, work—and the more we talked, the more I realised what a nice, sweet guy he was. He was a genuine person, a super-rare quality in the men of a big city like Delhi.

"Urm, I hate to be a nosy-parker but I'm really curious, how on earth did those strange stories about you and that molesting thing spread? I can't possibly imagine you, of all people, doing anything of that sort. I mean, I know I barely know you, but you just don't come across as even being capable of pulling off that stuff."

"The thing is you don't know me that well. I could be capable and you'd never know it."

I put my hands over my mouth. "Oh my God! Are you saying that the stories are true?"

"No, I'm not, and they *aren't* true. Just don't get carried away with the idea that someone who seems to be a nice guy can't pull stuff like that, that's all."

I looked at him questioningly, a little confused.

"But, no, I didn't do anything to deserve my reputation. It . . . erm . . . well, I was seeing someone from the office. She was married but separated and on the verge of divorce when I met her. She'd been through a pretty bad marriage and, well, one thing led to another and we fell for each other. Only, she said we had to keep it a secret because if her husband found out she was seeing someone, he would use it to get custody of their son. I hated all the sneaking around, but it was for a good cause, so I agreed to it. One night—it was our six-month anniversary—I was over at her place when her husband came in. He still had the keys to the place. We were . . . ummm, making out. The minute she saw him, she pushed me off and started screaming and abusing me. She ran to her husband and told him I'd been forcing myself on her. He started to bash me up . . . we fought. Then she flew at me and screamed at me for hurting him . . . and . . . well, I got out of there. The next thing I knew, this story was all over the town and she'd gotten back with her husband . . ."

"Why didn't you do something? Why didn't you tell anyone the truth?"

"I tried, but no one believes the guy in stories like these. I had to quit my job . . . and pretty soon, no one would even agree to see me for an interview."

"What did you do then?"

"Had to find something else to do for a living. I started writing small little features for magazines . . . and now I write about travel."

"But that's so unfair! Can't you do something about it?"

"Na-ah. It's too late now and, anyway, what *can* I do? I just feel happy that her kid is back with both his parents . . . and try to put it behind me."

It didn't look like he'd been too successful in putting anything behind him; the chip on his shoulder was showing.

"Those are the breaks, I guess. Usually, in our system, it's the women who get shafted. For once it was the guy . . . you know, the balance would have made me feel better if only *I* wasn't the guy in question."

"I'm so sorry . . . and now I feel even more of a worm for all the names I called you . . . really. Thanks so much for taking care of me . . ."

"You're welcome! Just don't make a habit of it. You're no lightweight!" Debu grinned, and I noticed his whole face relaxed for the first time that day. He had nice eyes which, though usually a little sad-looking, were now all lit up.

"Hey, by the way, I've been meaning to tell you, thanks for rescuing my car. Where is it now?"

"No problem. Luckily, the building guard saw you straggle in that day and told me you'd gone to work in the car. So I figured something must have happened to it. I went out the next morning, saw it still stuck on the road, and got a mechanic to haul it out. Something about a choked pipe. It should be ready by tomorrow."

"Great. I really owe you one."

I had to think about hooking him up with someone; he was too good to waste. Sadly, there were no sparks between the two of us. Maybe he was too nice or something. Besides, I had Rocky, anyway. Junaki? She'd be good—she likes these silent, brooding types!

11

The days before the pitch were as usual absolutely frenzied. Literally hundreds of layouts were printed, presented to the suits—the client servicing types—and discarded. It was a madhouse. And, of course, in the middle of all this, there were tons of other jobs to be finished as well. And I had to deal with Rocky too, who was getting increasingly sullen as I was working late and cancelling dates almost on a daily basis. Seriously, I didn't get it. There were enough evenings when he also had to stay late in office and blow me off, but I never took it personally. I understood that's just the way it is in the marketing profession.

Meanwhile, I also had to suffer through another meeting with Mr Mishra, who was now planning to launch a beauty product(!). Junaki had been press-ganged into it with me and Suzie was the suit on the business. We got late and our arrival for the meeting clashed with Mr Mishra's sacred lunchtime. His lunch had already been laid out on the table behind him and he was just about to start eating when we entered. Believe it or not, as he spoke to us, he kept turning around on his swivelling chair to sniff it sadly and then turning back again to give us looks of unspeakable anguish. The whole room was filled with the aroma of his *aloo chholey*, and my stomach rumbled protestingly throughout the meeting.

"So, *madam, yeh jo* product *hai . . . ye aapki skin ko nikhaarta hai . . . malai ki tarah* (Ma'am, this product makes your skin soft, like cream). *Jesht* a minute . . ." He picked up the intercom and dialed a number. "Mehta*ji*, *aap yaha aakar ajainsy ko* explain *kardeejiye* product *ke baare mein* (Please come and tell the agency about the product)." After replacing the receiver, he said to us, relief etched on his face, "Mehta*ji*, our technical expert, will come and explain the product to you. Meanwhile, I'll take lunch."

Mehta*ji* crowded into the already-packed cabin, his woolen suit showering whiffs of mothballs around. The combination of this with *aloo chholey* was not exactly appetising. We exchanged agonised glances as Mr Mishra turned around on his swivel chair and calmly proceeded to chow down his lunch with much smacking of lips. The three of us were transfixed by the phenomenon. As we followed every bite of his noisy lunch all the way down to his gullet, Mehta*ji* began droning and the *jugalbandi* continued until every last morsel of food had been ingested.

"I tell you, it was the funniest meeting I ever attended!" I told Rocky that evening. "I don't think I'll ever be able to separate *aloo chholey* from face cream in my mind after today." Just the memory of the meeting was sending me off into squeals of laughter.

Rocky smiled unwillingly. I had gotten held up in office

and was forty-five minutes late, not to mention that we were meeting after five whole days courtesy my crazy schedule.

"Anyway, listen. Shonali called and she's finally been transferred to Bombay." Shonali was my hotshot I-Banker friend who'd been wanting forever to move to Bombay for her dream job. She was pretty uptight and serious about her career, but pour some tequila into her and, bam, it woke up the party woman inside. "So I wanted to throw her a farewell party. I thought it'd be a great opportunity to get Junaki and Debu together."

"Why do you care so much about Debu anyway?"

"Because I was really mean and nasty to him and owe him one. Besides, he's a nice guy. He should be with someone. It's really awful what happened to him."

"Hmm . . . sure something else isn't going on? I don't like the sound of that guy."

Rocky had a tendency of being a teensy bit possessive. It had started to get on my nerves.

"Come on, Debu's perfectly nice."

"Ha, ha, you know what they say about nice guys, don't you? He's a loser."

"He is not, and I hate it when you call him that. Don't call him a loser."

"Any guy who gets whupped by a woman . . ."

"What happened to him was terrible, and you should be sympathetic about it instead of finding it bathetic."

"'Pathetic', not 'bathetic', *buddhu*!"

"Actually, 'bathetic' is what I said and it's what I meant. Go look it up in the dictionary!"

The Silver pitch was to get over on Thursday, which meant Friday was all free to rock. I decided to get some *biryani* and kathis as party food. Drinks were Rocky's department and I pretty much left him to it, after a reminder, to get some tequila for the guest of honour. I'd also casually popped over and mentioned the party to Debu a couple of days before.

"Oh good, have fun."

"Don't be stupid; you're coming too."

"Oh no, I'm not. I don't do parties."

"Come on, what are you, eighty? Live a little. I'm telling you, my parties are great. Maybe you'll meet someone . . ."

Debu looked up from his book, alarmed. "Are you trying to set me up with someone? Because I hate when that happens. Don't *set* me up."

"Me? Set you up? Whatever gave you that idea? I'm just throwing a farewell party for Shonali."

"Then how come I'm invited? I don't even know her, or for that matter any other friend of yours."

"Well, come to the party and you'll get to know them. If you don't show up, I'm going to land up here and bug you till you come."

"Glad you warned me. I'll just stay away from the flat then."

"If you do that, I'll faint by the lift again. Come on, don't be such a recluse, you old stick-in-the-mud. It's only a party, not an orgy. And if you don't have fun, you can always come right back here and stick your nose back into a book again."

"Man, you're such a pest. All right. I'll show up, but don't expect me to hang around."

"Ooh, we are going to be so honoured by thy holy presence, thy majesty."

The party was rocking by midnight. I'd forewarned Mrs Muhammed to insert her ear plugs, so that the Scorpions could play at full blast. Though it was still only March and pretty cold, I'd worked up quite a sweat. Rocky loved to dance and so did I, so we'd been boogieing all night. Shonali had already had way too many tequila shots and was seriously working the dance floor, gyrating like a dervish.

"Finally!" I spotted Debu. "There you are, at long last. I thought you'd run away from home, just to avoid—oh what was that concept again?—fun!"

"If you call getting smashed to the eyeballs and waking up with a headache fun, running away might just be the answer," Debu said. Thankfully, he was smiling.

"Come on, Grandpa, I'll make you the first drink and throw a few names at you. But, after that, you're on your own."

I made sure I introduced him to Junaki, among enough other people, so that he wouldn't suspect anything.

I was kept busy after that—making sure the *biryani* was served and that people got their ice and whatever else they wanted. I finally caught up with Rocky around one, when the music had moved to Bollywood, which always gets everyone in the room on their feet.

"About time," he complained.

"Sorry, you know how it is."

Rocky caught me and pulled me into a deep embrace. He smelled wonderful—Eternity, I think—and he was looking so sexy, my heart went pitter-patter. "Okay, no more running around looking after anyone else now. This is our song, ok?"

Daler was belting out *thunak thunak thun* and it was hardly romantic. We both burst out laughing as we began to sway together to our own tune. I looked around to see what everyone else was doing. Shonali was hanging out in a corner with some guy, busy in what looked like an earnest debate. She was standing with her arms akimbo—the way she does when enjoying a good argument.

Junaki—I despaired!—had slumped over at a table and gone to sleep. All by herself.

"Oh, good grief, just look at her. After all my plans for her and Debu. Uff!"

"He-ey, give her a rest! It's time for you to take the rest of the night off and pay attention to me."

"Sure, but it's such a waste."

"I told you the guy was a loser. He probably made her fall asleep."

I stopped dancing and stepped back, out of Rocky's arms. "Rocky, we can't keep having this conversation. Please don't call my friends names. Debu is not a loser."

"What, are you in love with him? How come you're always worried about him?"

"Just! He's a nice guy and a terrible thing happened to him and then I did something horrible . . . so I just feel like I owe him something . . ."

"Do it in your own time then," Rocky snarled. At the same time, someone said, "Oh, spare me your pity!"

Horrorstruck, I turned around to find Debu standing

behind me, looking all weird—the way you do when you accidentally whack your funny bone.

"I didn't mean it like that, Debu . . ." He had left, banging the front door behind him, followed by Rocky. *Now what do I do?*

I had to chase after Rocky, so I grabbed Shonali and told her to do me a favour and go calm Debu down.

"That writer guy? He's so opinionated!" she slurred.

"Since when has that been a problem for you, Miss Soapbox? Now will you please just go? I don't want him to go away upset, ok? I've got to go calm Rocky down."

I ran barefoot after Rocky all the way to the parking lot—not fun on a cold spring night.

"Wait up! Wait up!"

Rocky had popped open the car door by the time I caught up with him. "Rocky, sorry . . ."

"Yeah, yeah, you're sorry. You're the queen of apologies."

"No, I am really sorry. You were right, I should have paid more attention to us. Come on, now please come back."

"Only if you promise not to see that guy again."

"Who? Debu? Rocky, you must be joking. He's just a friend, I swear to you."

"Then you can stop seeing him."

"Don't be funny, I can't. I can't just stop seeing my friends like that. Be reasonable."

By the time he finally agreed to come back to the party, I had almost started wondering why I was trying so hard. Debu had come back too, with Shonali. I silently waved to her to thank her. She winked back and went back to trying to teach Debu salsa.

Heaving a sigh of relief, I turned to Rocky. "See? There's nothing going on. Now can we please stop fighting and start flirting?"

"Whatever you say," Rocky said, spinning me around and dipping me down in a bebop move.

12

"So, how did you like the party?" I asked Debu when I surfaced the next morning and went to his apartment. I was anxiously watching him to check if he still sounded mad at what he'd overheard.

"Fine."

"Are we still talking about the weather? I thought we'd moved past it."

"Oh, all right, it was the best party I've ever been to. I got drunk and danced on the tabletop and wore a lampshade for a hat."

"Ha ha ha."

"No, it was fun actually. Your friend Shonali is pretty opinionated though. She seems like one of those people who think everything is black and white."

"Why do you say that?"

"Well, everything with her was 'my way or the highway': people should do this, they shouldn't behave like that, there should be a death penalty, blah blah blah. She does dance well though."

"She is pretty argumentative. But I guess she could have hardly become a successful banker by being a wimp."

"More like by being an aggro know-it-all!"

"Yeah, well . . . did you get to hang out with Junaki?"

"Oh, sure, nice girl."

"Nice?"

"Yeah, you know, nice. Sweet. We chatted about cricket for a while. She's . . ."

"Don't tell me, let me guess . . . nice?"

"Yeah. Why?"

Romeo and Juliet this wasn't. Later, Junaki didn't sound all that caught up by Debu either, so I decided to hang up my matchmaking boots and move on. Mr Mishra's scintillating campaign for the face cream had to be cracked, after all.

The three of us—J, Suzie and me—were back at his office for the nth meeting, where—you got it—he wanted his product to come 'jooming in' with a scantily clad female. Suzie was patiently trying to explain to him that scantily clad women would not help him sell a cream to other women when his phone rang.

"*Halooo? Yeas? Haanji,* Rakeshji . . . *Kya hai na, abhi main madamon se ghira hua hoon, aap se baad mein baat karta hoon* (Right now I'm surrounded by women; I'll talk to you later)." J and I rolled our eyes at each other, while Suzie, burdened by her servicing role, kept a straight face.

Rocky's agency was doing the research for them and Rocky was there to present the findings the next day. As usual, it was a 300-slide-deep presentation and the conference room temperature was set to Polar levels. You could see ice forming in various corners. I was expecting penguins to come waddling into the room any minute. I started to shiver, a few hundred hours into the presentation. Mr Mishra, who was sitting on the other side of the table, noticed. "Are you feeling cold, my dear?"

"Ye . . . es a little . . ." My teeth were chattering so hard I could hardly get the words out. My mind had totally tuned out the endless presentations decades ago.

"Come here, my dear, and sit next to me. I will . . ." I couldn't catch the whole sentence.

I anyway obediently got up and went sat down next to him, waiting for the presentation to go on. I noticed Junaki making fluttering motions at me and Suzie gesturing wildly with her eyes. But I had no idea what they were twittering on about. Rocky glared at me. I sent him an apologetic smile for interrupting his presentation.

After the meeting, I happily strode across to Rocky and said, "Hi, sweetie. That went well."

"Don't 'hi, sweetie' me. I saw what you were doing."

"Huh? What?"

"What was with all that body heat stuff?"

"What? What are you talking about?"

Junaki and Suzie joined in, giggling. "Ha, ha, this dodo didn't even get it. Mishra*ji* offered you body heat, you dumbo! 'I will be giving you lots of the body heat.' And there you were—calmly walking across the room and sitting next to him!"

"What's WRONG with you, Kajal? What's with him? That lech, I'm going to KILL him." Rocky was all worked up.

"Shit! Calm down, sweetie, I'm sure he didn't mean anything by it. Oh God, Suzie, you and Junaki have the filthiest minds. Look, that's his idea of PC with a woman. I never even heard what he said; all I understood was that he wanted me to sit next to him for some reason."

"Boy, do you need a guardian angel," Suzie giggled.

"Come off it, you guys. I can take care of myself."

Rocky and I met up at the Garden of Five Senses that evening before dinner. It was one of those lovely spring evenings when the temperature is just right and the gardens are full of flowers. I was watching the sun set somewhere behind the Qutab Minar, feeling a huge sense of well-being steal over me . . .

"Kajal, I was really upset by what happened in the meeting today."

"Oh, Rocky, can we not argue about it just now? This place is so pretty and the evening is so wonderful . . ."

"I'm pretty upset. You're my woman and I hate it when people try to take advantage of you."

"That's sweet, but . . . hey, what do you mean 'you're my woman'?"

"You are my woman, right? I mean, we're together . . ."

"Of course, but all this 'my woman' jazz makes you sound like a cave man!"

"Well, every guy turns into a cave man when the woman in his life is being threatened."

"No one's threatening me, baby. I'm a big girl; I can take care of myself."

"I know. But I want to take care of you too. I want our

relationship to move to the next level."

I turned around to stare at him. I didn't know if I was ready for *that*!

"I want to be the guy who'll look after you all your life. I . . . I want to marry you, Kajal."

Oh, THAT next level!

"Rocky . . ." I didn't know what to say. I mean he did make my heart beat faster and all, he was really fun to be with—except when he was acting all Neanderthal. Ma was sure to love him, I was certain . . .

"I know it's early days yet, but I have a feeling that something is right. And we're not getting any younger."

I was a little insulted by that.

"When you feel that something is right, you don't want to waste any time, right?"

Heck! This wasn't shopping! This was about the rest of my life! If I jump the gun while shopping, at best I lose a thousand rupees. If I were to do it with this, I would have had a lot more at stake.

"Rocky, I . . ."

"I have a feeling we're meant for each other. And that you'll see that real soon. My folks are coming down to Delhi at the end of the month. I'd really like you to meet them."

"Isn't it a little early?"

"Well, not that I'm going to introduce you to them as their going-to-be-*bahu* or anything; I'll just introduce you as a friend. But I'm *dying* to introduce you. I'm sure they'll like you."

"Hmm."

But what if I don't like them, I wondered out loud to Debu later that night.

We'd gotten in the habit of popping by for a nightcap at the other's place after getting in from work or whatever.

"Don't be so paranoid, I'm sure you'll like them. Rocky's an ok guy."

"Yeah, but this is all moving a little too fast for me."

"It's never just right for girls. It's always either too fast or too slow. What's the matter, you don't like Rocky any more?"

"No, I do, but it's just getting serious very fast."

"What's the bad news? It's nice that he feels so strongly about you, no?"

I guessed so, but still felt under pressure every time I thought about the impending meeting with his parents.

Rocky didn't help either.

"So what are your parents like?"

Normal, like all parents. Of course, Mom is a little old-fashioned. Thinks women shouldn't work and all that. But she's a real sweetie.

Mom always thinks all girls are after me. Ha ha. In college, every time a girl phoned me, I'd have to answer a million questions: Who is she? Where is she from? What's her family like?

She'll be thrilled to meet you; she's been trying to get me married off since I was in college.

I told them that you'll be joining us for dinner, and that you're a friend.

"Won't they find it weird if I just barge in on a family dinner?"

No, no, they're really sweet that way. Anyway, it's their anniversary party. By the way, I told Mom you are twenty-five, in case she asks. She thinks girls who aren't married off by twenty-five are a little strange. Ha ha.

Dad is a real stickler for punctuality. He hates it if people are late. So do be on time, sweetie.

"Ok, I will."

13

'Copywriter of the Year' was a nice dream while it lasted. We didn't get the Silver account, even after all the work we'd put in. The client wanted an agency which didn't have any 'car experience' for a fresh perspective, and it was no use telling them that Junaki and I didn't have any 'car experience'. That's the way the advertising cookie crumbles.

Meanwhile, another new client who was building a hotel in Agra had come along and Junaki and I had to come up with the campaign. At least the assignments we were being given were much bigger—a sign that RKS was taking my work seriously.

"The client has fixed up tomorrow for the site visit, okay? We'll leave by the seven o'clock Shatabdi and come back by the four o'clock train. This is a really senior-level meeting, so please dress formally," Vijaya, the servicing director, briefed me.

"Oh. What time would we be back?"

"Seven, I surmise."

Terrific timing, as usual! It was the same day as the dinner with Rocky's parents. Junaki was down with a bad cold and was recuperating at her aunt's place. So there was no way I could skip the recce.

"Can we reschedule the meeting? I have something critical tomorrow . . ."

"Um . . . no. This is a really senior-level meeting. It's taken months for the client to arrange for everyone else to be available on the same day. Besides, I checked with RKS, you have nothing urgent on your plate anyway."

I didn't want to talk about the fact that my personal life was on the line now that I was finally starting to lose my rep as the party girl and was getting some serious work.

"All right. What time did you say we'd be back?"

"We'll be back by seven. And, seriously, dress formally, ok?"

Did she think I was deaf or what? I sighed gustily, "Ya ya, blah blah blah . . ."

"Don't give me that, I mean it. This is one of their most premium properties, and their entire senior team is going to be there. We don't want to make fools of ourselves, so we must look and act mature and senior."

"Ok, got it. Should I dye some of my hair grey too?"

I swear she actually seriously considered it for a moment! "Naaaah, it'll look too fake. Just pin it back and tie it up."

Geez, these servicing types really take life too seriously.

A 7 a.m. train from the New Delhi Railway Station meant leaving Gurgaon by five thirty at the latest. What a pain. You know, I can party with the best of them all night long, but mornings are not my thing, they've never been. I got up, half-dazed, at four thirty (Jesus Christ!) and then stumbled around looking for 'formal' clothes. The thing is that we—the creative types—usually hang out in either cool or hot clothes—normal temperature clothes are just not our thing. This morning, it was especially worse because I was getting ready for the evening as well. Gosh, I was already so tense about meeting Rocky's folks . . .

Finally, I managed to locate one black pencil-skirt—one of Shonali's cast-offs—and a white collared shirt. I put on the old-fashioned gold studs Grandma had given me, dabbed on dull-brown lipstick and scraped my hair back. God, could I look any more corporate=boring? I slipped on my only pair of low-heeled bright-red pumps and spritzed on a layer of Truth. I shoved in a sample bottle of Poison, a pair of long, sparkly earrings and one silver *payal* into my bag so I could glam up for the evening later. I debated carrying along a pair of heels, but figured they'd be too painful to lug around. My five feet six inches would have to do.

Vijaya had already called me thrice from the cab she was waiting in impatiently. "You're late!" she shot as soon as I entered the cab.

"Only fifteen minutes, will you relax?" No wonder servicing people get ulcers. She looked like a youthful hag in her grey trouser suit. A huge brown briefcase and her no make-up look helped the cause. She could actually look pretty if only she learnt how to make the most of herself. I considered telling her this, but then thought the better of it.

We reached the station in plenty of time. The client team was already waiting for us, and as I took in the sight of the senior management team, I shot Vijaya a dirty look. Every one of them was in jeans or chinos, T-shirts and sneakers. Vijaya shuffled off to make sickening PC with them while I hung back, waiting for my brain to kick-start.

Apart from the Taj and the Fatehpur Sikri, Agra as a city is a total washout. It's hot, dusty and dirty, with crowded streets. Thankfully, a swish Mercedes bus had been laid out for the site visit. I was looking forward to seeing the hotel. Rumour had it that the client had lavished enormous sums on the décor and that every room had a view of the Taj—a distinction no other hotel could claim.

I was bitterly shocked when we reached the hotel site though. It looked like construction was still going on. Vast piles of marble slabs and stones lay everywhere, while steel rods stuck out like porcupine quills. The walkway was anything but smooth and I hobbled along in my pencil skirt, stumbling more than once and cursing Vijaya under my breath. The skirt stuck to me in the heat as we wandered around the muddy grounds, discussing the future landscaping to be done. The entrance to the hotel was blocked by a pile of construction stuff and everyone had to actually step over that. It would have been unthinkingly easy in my usual work wear of jeans and sneakers, but right then it looked like a mountain to me because of the skirt. I sure was going to make an idiot of myself in my skirt, I thought, and took a giant, clumsy step sideways. This was accompanied by the sound of a loud RIIIIIIP. I felt a cold draft whoosh up my legs. Not daring to turn around, and praying silently, I put my hand behind me and felt about. The slit at the back of the skirt. It was ripped right up the back. It was barely covering my panties!

Everybody politely pretended to not have heard anything and we proceeded to clamber up and down narrow, unfinished hallways and dimly lit passages, I holding the rags of my skirt and my dignity in one hand behind me. There was no scope for taking notes, unless I could write holding my notepad between my teeth, a feat that I have tried many times since then without success.

The hotel rooms were a disappointment too. I was expecting something like the Villa Cipriani or the Palazzo Versace, in terms of décor. What we had there instead was something that looked as if an upholsterer had projectile-vomited all over it. Every inch of the surface of the walls, the ceilings and the floors was covered with a prickly embellished fabric. Nothing matched or even had a soothing contrast. Yuck—we were supposed to advertise this?

Thankfully, the Taj *was* visible from multiple vantage points—including the outdoor showers—in every room and looked gorgeous. In fact, seen from a serene and soon-to-be-air-conditioned environment, it looked more majestic and more beautiful than it does close up, what with the crowds, the touts and the pestering guides who surround you as soon as you enter its premises.

They actually served us a pretty great lunch, a welcome break from our prior meetings with them where they had typically forgotten to as much as offer us water. After all the *biryani*, *tandoori gobhi* and *kebabs*, I was almost in a coma during their drier-than-toast presentation. I got antsier as the day wore on thinking about the evening. What was I going to do about my slitty dress? I knew I wouldn't have the time to rush back all the way to Gurgaon to change. And I knew that even if I managed to swipe some time from our busy schedule, there would be no place in Agra where I'd be able to get something decent to wear.

At last I managed to snatch Vijaya away from the client and hissed to her, "Have you got a needle and thread?"

"No, what do you think I am, a roving tailor?"

"What do I do about my skirt? I can't keep wandering around like this, especially on a train."

"Who asked you to wear such a stupid outfit?"

"You! You were the moron who told me to dress formally," I snarled. "You better come up with a solution or else."

"Else what?"

"Else I'm going to screw up the work I do for this client."

I could too: I could make her life miserable by acting difficult. I'd never done it so far, but we creative types wield a huge amount of power over the servicing types. If we don't like someone, we can literally make his or her life hell. I figured I had a legit cause here.

Vijaya went away for a bit and came back with a fistful of safety pins. "Here."

"Who am I, Liz Hurley? Are you insane?"

"That's all I could manage. The hotel's not functional yet, so they don't have sewing kits here."

I went to the washroom and laboriously used the twenty or so mini-pins to pull the edges of my skirt together. It didn't look good at the end, but it did save my modesty and my hand from cramping. I could only pray that none of the pins would come undone and stick me in the tush. Anyway, it was a welcome relief to stop worrying about exposing too much. I could finally nap my way back to Delhi on the train, plotting to make a quick visit to the stalls at Janpath and buy something less perilous for the evening.

Of course the train had to run late the one time I'd taken it. We pulled into the station only at 8. Turquoise Cottage, where the dinner was, was at least 45 minutes away. There was no way I could go to Janpath, unless I wanted to be seriously late and look rude in front of Rocky's parents. I speed-dialled Junaki but no luck—she was at her aunt's in Old Delhi. I'd have to brazen it out. This was going to be one for the books!

14

The traffic was horrendous so I got quite late for the party. Quarter past nine. Rocky glared at me as I walked in.

"So sorry, I had gone to Agra from office and the train got delayed," I apologised in the best possible manner to his parents, a rather stuffy-looking couple. His mom was wearing a chiffon *sari* and a sleeveless blouse that revealed way too much doughy cleavage. Her hair was tied in a beehive bun that looked as if it hadn't been undone since her wedding day. She had an exaggeratedly colonial way of speaking that set my teeth on edge.

The entire table consisted of 'Golden oldies' and I wondered why they'd picked TQC for their party—IIC was more their speed. Rocky, his two female cousins and I were the only people in the party below 50. Rocky was looking amazingly hot as usual in his formal blue shirt and with that evening stubble that added a touch of roughness to his handsome face. And, of course, his gorgeous hazel eyes. Sadly, the chair next to him wasn't free and I had to sit across him, next to his mother and her impressive embonpoint. Every time she leaned over . . .

"What'll you have to drink?"

"I'm dying for some chilled beer," I told his father brightly. "This has been such a bad day. So have you people ordered? The food here is great; it's one of my favourite restaurants."

His dad stared at me strangely before calling a waiter to take my order. I felt a sharp kick on my ankle and looked over at Rocky to see him shaking his head and making surreptitious slicing motions with his hand against his neck. What was that all about?

The beer came pretty promptly and I chugged a good long draft of it, heaving a long, contented sigh. The table was utterly silent and as I gulped my mouthful of beer, I noticed that every single person at the table was staring at me. I finished my sip and looked around nervously. Then I noticed. Everyone else, even Rocky the Jockey, was having either a cold drink or juice. Ok, major gaffe there! My eyes fell on my cellphone where the message icon was blinking furiously.

Wat d hell r u doin??? They dont apprve of drnking!!!

Too late now. A little heads-up would have been nice. I had to think quick.

"What is this horrible stuff?" I exclaimed pointing to the beer. "It tastes foul."

"It's beer, madam," the waiter said.

"WHAT? Real beer? Are you crazy? I wanted fruit beer. Ewww, this tastes vile."

"Fruit beer? We don't have that here."

"Oh, then please take this away and bring me a nice, cold glass of milk . . ." *Ok, maybe that's going too far, idiot!* "Ermmm, I mean milk shake."

"We don't serve milk or milk shakes, madam. If you would prefer juice . . .?"

"All right then."

"I thought you frequent this restaurant?" Rocky's mom asked.

"Oh yes, I love this place. I'm here all the time."

"Funny you don't remember that they don't serve milk shakes," her voice tinkled like ice chips.

"Oh . . . ermm . . . I must have it confused with someplace else."

We went through the process of ordering, which was so slow and painful and debated over, you'd think this was their last meal before execution. Despite the heavy lunch, I was dying of hunger, so all this discussion was excruciating. The conversation was pretty boring too, all gossip about family and friends I'd never met:

Anila Auntie's finally going off on vacation. They'll take the Superstar Virgo cruise.

Oh, remember Nikhil? Well, he's completed his interior design course. Such a bright boy, though you know, a boy interested in interior design seems so frivolous!

Oh, have you heard about Shilpa? She's back in town from the US, and is looking even more beautiful. You must give her a call, Rocky. *She's so bright and yet so homely. She's even done her MBA. And she's such a great cook . . .*

And Rocky had turned into someone else right before my

eyes—a simperingly agreeable boy, who resembled Salman Khan from a Sooraj Barjatya movie, had taken over the party boy in him. He nodded in time with everything anyone said and did the whole '*Haanji* Auntie, *haanji* mummy' routine pretty convincingly.

There was a group of ad types at a corner table, clearly having a great time. They were laughing and chatting, their table laden with beer and appetizers. I knew some of them and they waved to me to come over, but I waved back forlornly. I was stuck with this boring family party for the evening. Oh well, hopefully it was for a good cause.

I was lapsing back into the comatose state from the afternoon when someone came and hugged me from the back. "Hey, Kajal, good to see you, *yaar*! Haven't met up in ages."

I twisted around to spot Nitin, a music composer whom I'd done a few commercials with.

"Hi, Nitin, what are you doing here? How are you, how's it going?"

"Great. We're actually playing here tonight. We've started getting gigs and all now. Come on, meet the band."

"Oh . . . maybe later. We've just ordered dinner."

"Come on, *yaar*, dinner will take a few minutes to come. *Chal*!" he practically dragged me out of my chair and across the room to where the band was setting up. They were nice guys and were together only for an evening gig. By day, they were merchant bankers, ad types and so on. You see, most rock bands don't earn much in India. I had some laughs with them and got back to the table, only to find open hostility on Rocky's face and a frankly disapproving expression on his parents'. The rest of the table looked on, vaguely shocked, apparently dazed.

"Oh, Nitin is someone I've worked with . . . heh, heh!" I weakly and hastily justified myself.

His parents said nothing; they just looked down their snooty noses at me. I noticed my message icon blinking again.

Wat d f r u wearing? These r my parents for God's sake.

Now the penny dropped. I had almost forgotten about my ripped skirt. I quickly dropped into my chair and launched into the story, "The most embarrassing thing happened to me today . . ."

No one looked sympathetic, though a few of the fuddy duddies did send an occasional and misplaced 'oh, ah' my way during the storytelling. Rocky's face continued to look tense and hostile, and I was really disappointed. This was supposed to be such a big step and everything so far had gone so wrong! I guessed I'd have to explain everything to him later and make it up to him somehow. I tried to be as unobtrusive as possible after that, quietly scoffing my dinner, while the boring conversation eddied on around me.

The band had started and they were pretty good. They were belting out rock numbers like "Stairway to Heaven" and "Hello, I Love You". I couldn't help dancing a little in my seat. I can never sit still when there's rock music playing.

"Hey, Rocky, want to dance?"

Rocky paled, looking nervously at his parents before replying, "No, I don't really enjoy this type of music. Too loud."

His parents nodded in approval, "Yes, we don't really like

this type of music. Lata, Asha, Rafi, Saigal, these are singers to listen to, not this rubbish."

Ok, I do love Asha and Rafi and Lata as much as anyone, but there's place for different kinds of music, no? Not to mention Rocky hadn't exactly been boogieing to Saigal tunes with me. I was starting to seriously dislike this new Mamma's-darling-Rocky.

"So . . . I believe you work in advertising?" Rocky's mother, this.

"Yes, I'm a copywriter."

"Copy what? You copy writing?"

"No, I mean yes, I mean, I write ads."

"Oh, how interesting. Must be a fun job, good timepass, not so stressful. Poor Rakesh! He has such a responsible job, dealing with all those important people as his customers."

I gritted my teeth. She was really wearing me down. "Well, it is a fun profession but I don't know about the not-so-stressful part. You see, we are responsible for crores of money that clients spend on their advertising."

"Come on, Kajal," Rocky, no, Rakesh chimed in. "Advertising is one of the easiest professions to get into. You don't even need a degree or anything for it, anyone can get in. You're anyway not that serious about it, are you? Once you get married and have kids, that's what you'll get busy with anyway. I mean, this is fun but it's not for the long term. Hey, that rhymed!"

I don't know if it was the lighting but Rocky suddenly became a lot less attractive and more ferret-like. I couldn't help but notice that his jawline was a little weak and that his teeth were too small. Funny I hadn't noticed that before.

"So are you—fun, but not for the long term. Have a nice life!" I said, and haughtily walked to the dance floor, all by myself. Nitin waved to me and I joined the band as they belted out "I Want to Break Free". Not only was it one of my favourite songs, but at the moment it was like my anthem. I let it rip, right from the heart, and barely even noticed when Rocky and Co. left the place.

15

Monday morning had rolled round again. Mondays are my lowest energy time of the week. Actually, my week tends to go like this: From Sunday afternoon onwards, my energy level starts depleting steadily and by Monday morning I'm almost in a state of coma. Till about Wednesday I'm pretty much the same way. Friday night is when I'm at my perkiest best. A lot of my best lines make an appearance on the dance floor on Friday evenings.

I tossed a bleary look at the alarm clock and settled down for a much-needed five-minute snooze. I'd recently read in a comic strip that the amount of sleep the average person needs is always ten minutes more. I couldn't agree more. Half an hour later, I'd finally dragged my carcass out of bed into the shower, hoping some cold water would get the old adrenalin going.

A bleak hour later, I trudged into the office, my brain still asleep. I was late as usual. People used to sharpen their wits at my expense about this when I'd first joined, but they gave up a long time back. Not that I cared—I put in enough late nights!

I got a sugar rush from the machine coffee. It energised me enough to pay attention to what's being discussed. A game of ping-pong—otherwise known as job review meeting—was in full flow.

Listen, we have a pitch in four days. We better have some creative ready by tomorrow.

Ya, ya . . . you guys gave us a brief on Friday afternoon. Whaddya think, we don't need any time off?

The brief was shit as usual. How do you expect us to come up with anything?

The brief was fine, you guys just don't want to stretch; everything has to be handed on a silver platter to you.

Yeah, baby, that'll be the day.

Suddenly the conference room door banged open and RKS walked in.

"Guys, I'm glad we're all here. Good news. I met the JRH people yesterday. They're planning a new product launch. And we're one of the agencies they're considering."

"Hey, that's a good news. How big is the account?"

"It's gonna be big. Those guys are really ambitious. They have a 'Number One or Two Rule', you know. In every market they enter, they want to be either number one or number two, and they're more than willing to spend whatever it takes to achieve that goal. This could be the turnaround opportunity we've been waiting for! We haven't won a pitch in a while."

"What are they launching?"

"Condoms. I have sample packs here. Obviously this is a category where there really isn't anything very different about the product. What we have to crack is a unique marketing approach. Guys, I'm very excited about this. I've handled the JRH account before and these guys are dynamic. If we handle this pitch well, we could walk away with a lot more business."

"When's the pitch?"

"We have six weeks and it's a clean slate. Everything, including the brand name, is up to us."

He left us to it in the conference room, which instantly became abuzz with excitement. Ad agencies get easily excited, and this was a really big opportunity, capital B-I-G. JRH was a huge multinational conglomerate and they made everything from food products to detergents to, now, even condoms. Not only this, they were also one of the country's largest advertisers.

Everyone wanted to be on the pitch. There was nothing like top management involvement to generate enthu.

And, of course, this offered a great opportunity for mock-leers and non-veg jokes. The guys were quickly hard at it (no pun intended) and started horsing around with the sample packs. A condom was taken out and was blown up like a balloon.

How about this for a marketing brainwave? Let's sell them as party décor—flavoured balloons.

Hey, how about better flavours like tiramisu or something?

One of the condom packs was tossed my way. "How 'bout a woman's point of view, eh?" Suraj, the tosser, asked. "What's your favourite dessert?"

"Yeah, sure. Just read Cosmo and you'll know all about it."

"No, seriously, I think it might be interesting for us to have a woman in the team. It'll make them sit up during the presentation for one thing."

Should I become the AGD (Attention-Getting Device) for the pitch? *No! Or, maybe, yes? It would be a good opportunity to grab the spotlight, and heaven knows I've been feeling rather like a mushroom lately. Yes, yes. Totally, yes.*

"Okay, I'll do it."

Junaki, of course, squealed like a stuck pig when I told her. "What were you thinking, K? How embarrassing! How are we going to do this campaign?"

"No problem, *yaar*, we'll just read up on the research and do some poking around—pun unintended. I'm sure we'll manage to dig up something."

"Still, sheesh. Imagine telling your parents you're working on condoms."

"Sometimes you can be such a BTM! Grow up, babes."

16

"KAAAJAL! Oh my God, you're here at last, yippee!"

"Shonali! Yippeee!"

I was in Bombay for a film shoot and had come to stay with Shonali, instead of going to the fleabag hotel the client had arranged. Of course, the shoot was going to come in the way of the condom campaign but that was ok—it never pays to be ready too far in advance in advertising.

Shonali lived in a—let's face it, despite it being a bank flat—two-bedroom little matchbox. The whole house could have fitted into my Gurgaon apartment's drawing room, but at least it was in the supposedly hip, upmarket Bandra. Shonali and I went cruising in her Swift that night, driving past Pali Hill where she pointed out Salman Khan's and Sanjay Dutt's apartments. Sadly we didn't actually spot anyone famous, but we did make it to the Prithvi Theatre and stood in line for their famous Irish coffees.

"What's up with life, man? Found anyone new yet, after Rocky?"

"Nope, and not even looking. Right now I'm on a mission

to get somewhere in my career. I have this campaign to do on a new brand of condoms . . ."

"Haha, you advertising types really lead a crazy life."

"How's it going with you? Are you seeing anyone here? How's life in Bombay?"

"Oh, life is pretty hectic here. Run, run, run—from early morning to late at night. I have a bunch of friends here, though no one as close as the Delhi gang. And with all the commuting, who has the time for romance?"

"That's too bad."

"Oh, well, it's ok for now. How's it going with you and that argumentative friend of yours? Debu?"

"It's fine, he's cool."

"So are you guys getting together?"

"Good grief, no way! He and I are just friends. God knows why, Rocky also jumped to the same conclusion. You know how it is—some guys just don't do it for you. Though he's a nice guy and all, we're just good friends, really. I thought Junaki and he would hit it off, but no dice. So Monsieur Hermit plods on . . ."

"I thought he was pretty interesting."

"Uhuh . . . maybe I should get the two of you together sometime."

"No way, who has the time for all this *makkhi-maarna*?"

The shoot was as hectic as they go, especially because it was the monsoon. Every morning, I'd wake up early and dash to the window to see if it looked like rain. Since the film was set outdoors, even a hint of cloud could throw us off schedule; a drizzle was a complete calamity.

After several delays, we finally managed to squeeze the

shoot between two consecutive sunny afternoons. I took Shonali out to Olive in Bombay to celebrate. The restaurant looked magical, all in white, with the pebbled courtyard and the twinkling fairy lights. I could easily imagine myself in another world, somewhere on a Greek island, the only thing missing being an Adonis.

Shonali and I downed some exquisite Cabernet Sauvignon while leching around at the male eye-candy. Olive is *the* place to go on Thursday nights—the day when all the wannabe movie-stars and starlets as well as many male models end up there. For a second, I even thought I spotted Sachin Tendulkar there, but I was too busy enjoying the glorious sunset to care. Plus, frankly, by that time I had begun to doubt my ability to walk and think straight.

They had an amazing selection of food on the menu. It took us really long to go through it because the words were jigging up and down before our eyes. Shonali, who was way more adventurous about food than I was, went for the oysters. I stuck to the good old pasta. The order came in no time.

"Uff, sometimes you can be so boring!"

"What's boring about pasta? Tastes great, doesn't it?"

"Yaa, but there are so many other things you could have tried here. Okay, you have to have one oyster."

"No, yuckkk, they're all slimy."

"No, I insist. It's high time you stop being so judgemental. What's the worst that will happen? You won't like it. No? See, here," and she put an oyster in my plate.

"Oh God, it looks so . . . wriggly. How on earth do I take it out of the shell?"

"Just use these tongs and pull gently."

Well, I did just what I was told. I promise. But given my klutzy genes, the oyster went flying right off the tongs, just like in *Pretty Woman*, and landed inside some guy's drink at the next table.

"What the F . . .?"

"Whoops, sorry, so sorry . . ." I turned around, face beet-red, to apologise to the guy. He looked mad as hell, but also kind of cute, and also, erm . . . kind of familiar.

"Dhir?"

"Huh? Do I know you? Wait a minute! You're the girl who hides under tables!"

Hmm, not exactly the way one likes to be remembered by a handsome guy, but it was a start alright. As everyone at his table began looking at us curiously, Shonali began exchanging hi-hellos with them.

"Hey, hi, Shonali!"

"Hi, Dhir, how's it going? You and Kajal know each other?"

"In a manner of speaking, yes, though I just found out her name thanks to you. Why don't you guys join us?"

Shonali and I shuffled over and made ourselves comfortable. I'd snagged a spot next to Dhir but now it felt a little funny sitting next to him. I felt little shivers of excitement but also wondered whether we'd find anything to talk about at all.

"Hey, you owe me a drink, having oysterized my last one!"

"Oh, right, sure, name your poison."

"Just kidding. I was going to order another martini, anyway. What can I get you?"

We settled down with our martinis. The conversation on the table eddied around the latest movies, stories from I-banking and so on.

"So what brings you to Bombay?" Dhir asked me, when the others had begun talking about something neither of us was interested in.

"A film shoot."

"Wow, any celebs?"

"Yeah, Shah Rukh."

"No kidding, really? What's he like?"

"A complete pain in the ass. For a five-year-old, that kid sure knows how to get on your nerves and then stay there. By the end of the shoot, the director was pleading to be allowed to slip some arsenic into his cola!"

"Haha, very funny, for a moment I thought you meant The Shah Rukh Khan!" After a momentary, uneasy pause, he said, "You know, erm, I've thought about you off and on . . . but didn't know how to get in touch."

"Yeah, right. Spin me another one."

"It's true. I even told my best pal Jeet all about how we met. You see it's not everyday a beautiful chick literally falls at your feet!"

I poked him and gave him a dirty look, but was secretly quite pleased with how this was going. I could feel the resident butterfly in my stomach, delivering her tiny tipsy babies at an unprecedented speed.

"So how did it go with the Neanderthal you were trying to avoid that night?"

"Hmmm, I find it pretty easy to stay out of his way, except

when Mom comes into town. How about you—did you date the Karol Bagh Auntie or Sharon Stone?"

"Neither, thanks very much. I have better taste . . . like you, for example."

Hmmm . . . coming on pretty strong for a second meeting. But I like it.

"You don't waste much time, do you?"

"We've wasted a good six months already, right?" An enchanting smile later, he continued, "So how long are you here? Any chance we can meet up again?"

"I'm leaving day after, evening. I'm supposed to meet up a bunch of old college pals tomorrow. Besides, we're meeting right now," I said, gesturing around the table. It had turned pretty raucous—everyone clearly had had a lot to drink. Some seriously off-key attempts were being made to karaoke along with the jazz songs playing.

"Yeah, well, this isn't what you'd call an ideal setting, no? Maybe if I could mute these guys, or even better, make them disappear. Seriously, are you free tomorrow?"

"I'm meeting my pals for a drink around seven and I have some work to wind up in the morning. Maybe a late-ish drink/ dinner?"

"Sounds good. You think we can meet up around eight?"

No point playing hard to get when you're already living over a 1000 kilometers apart. "I'll try. Why don't I call you when I'm done with my friends?" I said, trying to keep my face neutral. You don't want to scare off a guy with too much enthu.

17

Of course, all day, apart from the meeting with the film producer who wanted to discuss the edit, the only thing I could do was think of Dhir. He made my knees weak, just like the Mills & Boon heroes did to their heroines. What a pity he lived in Bombay!

I dressed really carefully for my evening out. I didn't want to look like I'd made too much of an effort but I also wanted to blow his socks off. I rummaged through Shonali's closet and the remaining dresses in my suitcase that were still clean. I finally pulled out a cotton dress I had picked up from a roadside store. It was a melange of purples, blues and greens mixed like watercolours and had delicate little straps. It made my skin luminous. I smoothed on Shonali's tinted moisturizer to add the right sheen to my face and wore my favourite silver, fish-shaped earrings. I picked up a silver scarf, just in case the restaurants were cold and slipped my feet into a pair of strappy silver sandals which I had brought from Mango. I actually went to the trouble of blow-drying my hair, so it behaved and swung out in measured waves instead of its usual untamedness. A dab of nude lip gloss and a touch of mascara later, I was good to go. I looked pretty good, if I do say so myself, as I walked out of the apartment in a cloud of Amarige by Givenchy.

I was meeting my friends at Mondegar's, for old times' sake. I was the first one to reach the place and felt a bit stricken as I kept stealing glances at my mobile, waiting for the others to turn up. It was past 7:30 by the time they all showed up to meet an antsy me.

It was great catching up with the gang, but I couldn't focus on the conversation. I was too eager to meet Dhir. It was unlike me, because I firmly believe girl pals are as important, if not more, as boyfriends (and they are more permanent too!). But that time I was really on pins and needles and just dying to get out. Finally, I couldn't stand it any longer and stood up to go at 8:15.

"Hey, don't leave us already!" Nina called out, yanking me back down.

"I'm really sorry but I have a dinner date," I blurted out. I couldn't lie to these gals, we shared too much.

"Oh, so you're blowing us off for a guy?" Diana said accusingly.

"I'm so sorry, but it just suddenly came up . . ." I trailed off guiltily.

"Just pulling your leg, *yaar*. It has to be an important one, otherwise you wouldn't blow us off. Who's it?"

"I'll tell you guys later. I have to rush." A quick round of hugs and I was off. I called Dhir and found he was in the vicinity, as we'd planned. He met me outside the restaurant. He looked gorgeous, with a hint of late evening stubble, and I felt shivers running down my spine. I couldn't stop staring at him.

"You look amazing," Dhir said.

I'm really bad with responding to compliments, so I just blushed.

"I've been looking forward to this all day. It seems like every time we meet, there's an unfinished conversation."

Hey, he'd read my mind!

He casually reached out and grabbed my arm and we started off down the road. It was crowded with the usual roadside hawkers and the pavement was rough as hell on my stilettos, but I was too bemused to mind such trivialities.

We arrived at a gorgeous restaurant right on Chowpatty Beach. Little secluded tables were set up in the sand and the seats were sink-into, four-poster *divans*. Sheer white curtains fluttering in the sea breeze screened off each table, but the roof was open to the dark monsoon clouds surrounded by billowy rose-tinted ones—a result of the amazing sunset playing out across the sky. Candles set into small little glass holders on each table twinkled, casting a sparkling aura of dim light on the magical surroundings. The waves hushed back and forth dreamily on the shore, tinted here and there with a rosy colour fallen from the sky.

A waiter bustled up and served us something out of a bottle as I sank down and took in the setting.

"Cheers to finally getting together," Dhir said, picking up his glass after handing mine to me. I crooked my arm around his and we took in a deep draught.

"Champagne?!" I sputtered in surprise.

"What else would I use to celebrate this moment?" Dhir grinned and I grinned back, downing the rest of my glass. Not MDP, but French champagne, no less.

I didn't feel like making the effort, so Dhir ordered for both of us. Course followed course—lobster mousse, asparagus salad with goat cheese and pine nuts, cheese soufflé . . . I suppose everything tasted fantastic because we sent away a lot of empty dishes, but I can't remember exactly. All I can remember is how Dhir tasted when he took a bit of the soufflé on his finger and fed it to me and how we fed each other tiramisu with our hands and how we laughed and talked about our pasts and about our dreams for the future and how the candles had guttered down to almost nothing in their holders and the waiters had packed away all the other tables by the time we realised we had to leave . . .

A cab pulled up and we got in for the long ride to the suburbs. I hoped it could somehow take forever; I didn't want that magical night to end. As the driver let in the clutch, Dhir pulled me close to him and I snuggled up to him in that intimate silence that happens when you know there's magic in the air. He curled his arms around me and rested his chin on my hair as I leaned back on him. I swear that could have been my definition of 'heaven'.

We watched the yellow-washed streets of Bombay flash past us in rapt silence. After a long, long while, Dhir said, "I have to see you tomorrow. You can't just go back to Delhi like this."

I turned my head back to look at him, "I've been trying not to think about that."

"Well, you still have one day left. Spend it with me."

"Don't you have to work?"

"Work? What's that?"

"Seriously!"

"This is way more important than work. You know that, right?"

I nodded solemnly. I couldn't find the words to explain what was happening to me, but it felt as if whatever was there between Dhir and me was going to change my life.

"Come on, spend tomorrow with me. It'll be our day of grace. A day stolen away from everything else, a day just for us."

Day of grace. I liked that.

We pulled up outside Shonali's apartment building and Dhir had the taxi wait while he dropped me off.

"Just drop me at the lift," I pleaded. I needed a few minutes to compose myself before going up to meet Shonali's eagle-eyed gaze.

We paused when we reached the lift, neither of us willing to let the evening be over. Dhir held both my hands and pulled me close, and I melted into his embrace. He put his hand under my chin and lifted my face up towards his and slowly, ever so slowly, lowered his lips to mine. It was the sweetest, gentlest, tenderest and yet the most exciting kiss that I had ever experienced, and I wished it could go on forever, even as we reluctantly came up for air. As he looked down at me, there was a look in Dhir's eyes that I don't remember ever seeing in any man's eyes before, and later, when I thought about it, I realised that I had lost my heart to him in that instant. Dhir cupped my face in his hands and dropped a kiss on my hair before tearing himself away, saying, "I'll pick you up at ten."

I looked out after him, all the way till his taxi pulled away and the tail-lights were mere pinpricks in the distance. I felt all awash with emotion, thrilled inside and yet strangely feeling as if I were outside my own body. I wanted to relive each moment of our evening together and yet I didn't want to think about it; it was too raw. I couldn't remember ever having felt so strongly about anyone before, and I wondered what this was about as I touched my lips to see if I could still feel his lips on them . . .

18

I have an unfortunate problem: everything I'm thinking gets printed on my face and can be easily read by people who know me well. I knew I couldn't afford to run into Shonali right then for she'd jump to it in no time and pester me for details and all that. I just wasn't ready to deal with it right then. Had it been a JLT date with someone, I'd have surely loved to stay and chat and laugh about it. But this . . . I didn't even want to call it a date. It was nothing that I had ever experienced before. It was something totally new: so fragile, so easily breakable, like a soap bubble.

I needed to hide it away, so I stopped at the foot of the stairs and took a deep breath, willing myself to concentrate on everyday normal things—the stink of the garbage piled up just outside the lobby, the hideous condom campaign that I had still not cracked, a client's impending approval of the film shoot I'd just supervised, my overdue and overburdened credit card bill, the fact that my flat would probably need a major clean-up when I got back, the fact that my periods were due next week—anything to wipe the exhilaration off my face. I pulled out my compact mirror and stared at myself. Shit, my face was still glowing from that kiss. Come on, Kajal, focus! My cell started ringing in my bag and I fumbled for it among all the debris inside. Seriously, sometimes I think my handbag could qualify for an archaeological treasure. It needs excavation at minimum!

"Hello, ya, Shonali?"

"Listen, where are you? When are you back? I need to crash early, got a really early morning meeting tomorrow."

"I'm almost home . . ."

"Anyway, I've left the key hidden in its usual place, ok? I'm heading to bed right now, gotta get up at six. What time's your flight tomorrow?"

"Seven o'clock."

"Shit, ya, that means I wouldn't be able to come to see you off also. You should have stayed home today instead of going off with your college pals. We could have hung out . . ."

"Sorry, but today was the only day they were free. I'll see you in the morning *na*?"

"Don't bother, I'll leave by 6:30. Just leave the key inside and pull the door shut when you leave, okay? I'll call you during the day tomorrow, maybe we can have lunch?"

"Ya, that sounds nice. *Chal*, good night and thanks for a lovely stay."

"G'night."

Thank God, she was off to bed! I wouldn't have to lie through my teeth! I felt bad about not being able to see her before leaving for Delhi and I already knew I wouldn't be able to make it for lunch the next day either. It was the last day I had with Dhir. I hung around the staircase for another ten minutes to ensure Shonali was off to sleep. The guard threw me a couple of puzzled looks and finally asked me, "*Kya hua*? Aren't you staying at Flat No. 26? *Didi* is already home."

"Yes, I know but I'm . . . I'm . . . waiting for something."

The lift was out of order, as usual, but I was too elated to mind it. I climbed the stairs to the flat and felt above the door for the spare key. Gingerly I unlocked the door and crept into my room. Phew!

As I lay down to sleep, I couldn't help remembering each and every word of the conversation between Dhir and me, especially Dhir's lines and the way he said them and the way he looked while saying them. There was no doubt he liked me, we were way past that. I remember how, back during college time, any time you were interested in a guy, you would never be sure whether he liked you back and you would try to find out through nefarious, tortuously slow means: one of your friends would chat with one of his, one of your friends would then hit on him, you would then painstakingly ignore him for a while, and so on and so forth.

Thank God we were clear about that. What I wanted to figure out was how much I liked him. Was this IT? Certainly the resident butterfly in my stomach was going crazy like never before with her babies. I could still feel his kiss, soft and light as it had been, on my lips. I was really excited about our next day together. But after that, what? I'd be back in Delhi, he in Bombay. How would we make this long distance thing work? I was not much of a letter writer, and somehow I felt that trying to make it work on the phone or email would be too much of a hassle.

What if we build up unrealistic images of each other, through emails or whatever, and it didn't work out when we actually met? That had happened to me before with friends. Once people move away, you can't really keep up with everything going on in their lives, and then when you meet after a year, you sit like a couple of lame ducks, scratching around for something to talk about and finding nothing in common. This has happened to me even with people I grew up with and spent most of college glued to the phone with.

Nope, no good at all. I just couldn't tamp down my feelings of excitement about Dhir—there was way too much adrenalin in the system. No point trying to be realistic when you are living around your fantasy.

Unsure of what to feel and think, I made a decision: "No more thinking about all the negative possibilities." I was just going to go with the flow and see what happened. This was possibly the best thing that had come my way and I couldn't possibly throw cold water on it. I'd deal with the consequences when they happen. Far better to have loved and lost and all that jazz . . . I drifted off to sleep with a giant smile on my face.

Shonali poked her head in way too early in the morning to say bye. A quick hug and a whiff of Dune and she was out. I couldn't sleep any more after that, so I got up and had a leisurely cup of tea, staring out at the Bombay monsoon. It had been raining steadily throughout the night, and the air was cool and damp, though the underlying mugginess could still be felt. In Bombay, it never quite goes away. I packed in a hurry and then got into the bath. I had all the time in the world for a long, leisurely soak, since Dhir was supposed to pick me up only by ten. The doorbell started buzzing at a quarter past nine, and I rose from the tub, grumbling. Why was I never fated to enjoy a soak?

Grabbing a towel around me, I raced to the front door and banged the door open for the *bai* who was usually late on rainy mornings. I had already turned back towards the bathroom when it registered. It was Dhir!

"What are you doing here so early?" I cried in shock.

"I couldn't wait to see you any longer."

"Oh . . ." I could feel a bright red blush stealing over my face. "Hmm, I'll just finish my bath. Help yourself to a coke or something if you'd like," I said before rushing back to the bathroom where my suspicions were confirmed—I had my hair up in its usual Narad muni style for a tub bath and my skin was all red and covered in bubbles. Not to mention the towel must have left way too much of my thunder thighs exposed. My bad. Very bad.

I hurried through a shower—ditching the hair-wash and blow-dry routine I had planned—and got dressed. My favourite pair of jeans, which made my butt look J-Lo-ish, and a white Mango T-shirt with a denim vest was my outfit for the special day. I put on my chunky silver hoops and did my face in its day mode—powder, *kajal* and pale lipstick. A spritz of Escape and I was good to go. But I lingered in the room, hunting for excuses not to go back out there. I was feeling totally mortified by Dhir's having caught me literally with my pants down!

"Kajal?"

No escape; had to get out there. "Just coming . . ."

"Ready to go?"

"Yup, let me take my bag, and I want to leave a note for Shonali . . . there."

We let ourselves out of the flat, Dhir carrying my backpack, and pulled the door shut. It was then that I looked at him properly for the first time that day. He looked scrumptious in a red, striped shirt, a pair of blue jeans and Levi's sneakers. A hint of stubble flecked his chin. I had a mad urge to reach up and feel the stubble, and I swear I had to consciously hold my arm down. He had a hint of laughter in his voice as he said, "I preferred you in the towel." And, suddenly, both of us were laughing.

"Come on, let's get going, we don't have too much time," he said, and we ran down the stairs two at a time. We stowed my backpack in the dicky of his Santro and got into the car in a hurry, as the rain had suddenly started whooshing down heavily.

"Where are we going?" I asked as I belted up.

He looked a little uncertain as he replied, "Well, the thing is, I really want to just hang out with you, get to know you a little better. So I thought . . . erm, if you don't mind we could just . . . go hang out at my apartment? If you're not comfortable, we can go elsewhere, just name the place . . ."

It sounded like a great idea to me—to spend time in a quiet place without hordes of other people and the constant fear of running into someone either of us knew. This felt too new and too precious to be out on public display just yet. "Sure, let's go!" I said happily, and he let in the clutch.

His place wasn't far but the rain had seriously slowed down the traffic. It felt snug to be cocooned in the tiny car, windows closed against the pelting water and passers-by reduced to blurry shapes. As he pulled away from the building, one of my favourite old songs, '*Pal pal dil ke paas . . .*', began playing on the radio. We both started singing it at the same moment, and our voices blended into a pleasing harmony.

When we reached his apartment complex, it seemed so natural for him to reach for my hand and lead me to his flat. He fumbled with the key when we reached his flat because he was holding my wrist in his right hand . . . Neither of us wanted to let go of each other's touch. I helped him and we together unlocked the door. Soppy, no?

I took a deep breath before I walked in.

See, I had this pet theory about guys' apartments. There were three variants:

1. The super messy, sloppy types, where things are strewn around, there's hardly any furniture, but there's definitely a general, musty, dank smell pervading the place. Guys like these aren't ready for commitment, they're just horsing around.
2. Then there's the other extreme, which looks like something out of a décor magazine. The guy has his cook and maid and furniture and knick-knacks, and everything is well-organised. Such guys have gone way beyond marriage, and while they may be

a lot of fun, they're just good for flings, because, heck, they have grown way too comfortable with themselves.

3. The third kind is the one with promise—it's a bit in the middle. It may be cluttered but it's not dirty, and it has a reasonable amount of furniture and organisation but not too much. Such guys are neither too cavalier nor too demanding. They're just perfect.

Phew! Dhir's apartment was just right (am I starting to sound like 'Goldilocks and the Three Bears'?). He had a *divan* and a couple of wicker chairs in his L-shaped living room. Clearly, a guy who loved and splurged on his entertainment, he had a 42-inch LCD TV, a JBL music system and a stack of DVDs next to his Sony DVD player. An untidy heap of magazines and newspapers lay on the floor next to the *divan*. The upholstery was a faded off-white, and the tumbled yellow-and-green cushions did not match the red-and-blue curtains. The place looked like it was swept and swabbed regularly. There were a couple of nice prints on the wall too—Klee's Castle and Sun and the quirky Cows by American artist Daniel Kessler. The place didn't have that horrible mustiness of unwashed clothes that many bach-pads have. An open kitchen with bright-orange cabinets was on the left and a dining table in the corner.

Dhir tossed his car keys onto the kitchen counter and said, "Make yourself at home." I wanted to tell him the same thing—he sounded stilted and we were back to awkwardness.

"Hmm . . . nice place. I have the same print at my place."

"Wow, cool. Want something to drink—coke, beer?"

"I'd kill for tea right now."

"O-kay, not one of my specialties but I'll try."

"Why don't I help?"

I didn't want to come over all domestic or anything but tea was something I really craved at the time. It would have been even more wonderful to get *pakoras* with it in that rainy weather, but, no, we had decided to come here where there was no service! I certainly wasn't going to psych him out by getting all kitchen-ey.

The kitchen was small and sparsely stocked: tea, coffee, soft drinks, some juice, vodka, breezers, beer, a couple of packets of chips, a pack of cornflakes and half a loaf of bread. Two rotten apples lay in the fridge next to the carton of milk and eggs. An unopened packet of *basmati* rice and *arhar dal* lay in a corner and a few old onions were still in their plastic bag.

"You usually eat out, huh?"

"Yes, I get out from work late, so I pick up something near office before heading home. Or I order in. I tried keeping a cook, but with my schedule it doesn't work out."

The tea was almost done and I handed Dhir the strainer. I had just turned around to find some teacups when whoosh! I was deluged with hot tea—right on my bum!

"Yaaaiiii!"

"I'm so sorry, SO SORRY . . ."

"Where's the bathroom?!"

Dhir pointed and I ran and locked the door behind me to quickly strip off my jeans and pour cold water on the afflicted area. It really hurt and I had tears of pain in my eyes even after I eventually came out, the sole damp towel from the loo wrapped around my waist. Pulling on the jeans would have hurt too much, besides they were soaked in tea. I had had to wring them out and hang them up, hoping they would dry by the time I had to leave.

Dhir was anxiously waiting for me right outside the loo, a tube of Burnol in his hand. "I'm so so sorry, I'm such a klutz! Is it hurting very badly?" he asked concernedly.

"It was pretty painful but it's getting better now," I said. He still looked very worried, so I clowned, "Hey, if you really liked me in the towel all that much, all you had to do was ask!"

We both collapsed on the floor and giggled and guffawed. Each time one of us would stop, we would catch each other's eye and start off again. Finally we stood up, weak-kneed with laughter, and Dhir put his arm around me. "Come on, I think the tea is done."

He sweetly ran out into the rain to get my bag up so I could change into a skirt and then we spent the whole day curled up on his *divan*, talking about anything and nothing. The dark grey sky and the pouring rain made us feel totally isolated, as if the two of us had been spirited away to a deserted island somewhere. He told me funny stories about growing up in a small town and I talked about Bunty. We even drifted off to sleep for a while, snuggled together, his head resting on mine.

Shonali called up at one, wanting to meet up for lunch or coffee, and I had to put her off.

"Come on, ya, God knows when you'll come here again. *Chal*, I'll take a long lunch break and we can go to Indigo."

I was all the way in Bandra. There was no way I could have gone across town in half an hour even if I wanted to.

"I've got some stuff to finish. It's ok, *yaar*, I'll be here again. Thanks a ton for the lovely stay."

"Oh ho, come *na*, don't be such a goof. What are you so busy doing?"

I frowned at Dhir, who was making yapping gestures at me.

"I just have some shopping to do—you know, take gifts home, buy books from Strand book stall, all of that. And I want to make sure I leave for the airport in plenty of time. It's raining so hard, I'm sure the traffic will be slow as molasses . . . Ouch!"

Dhir had started tickling me and I am an extremely ticklish person. "What ouch? What happened?" Shonali's voice echoed down the phone as I managed a "Talk to you later, . . . before I take off" and hung up and launched my revenge attack on Dhir. I found that he was as just ticklish as I was, and a breathless tickle-fight ensued all over the living room. I ran for the *divan*, Dhir close behind me, and he succeeded in grabbing both my arms behind my back, just as I collapsed onto the *divan*. Dhir fell on top of me, and as if it happened in slow motion, I looked up to find his face inches from mine, a question writ in his eyes.

Inevitably, we melted into each other. His kisses were delicious, warm and soft, trailing little feathers of excitement up my spine. I felt like I was flying up into a glorious blue sky, free and untrammeled, as I kissed him right back with every ounce of emotion I was feeling. My heart was beating frantically in time with his as we traded kisses. We had lost all sense of time and place by the time, centuries later, we pulled our lips apart and came back to earth.

19

I was still lost in his eyes, when a giant flash of lightning followed by the loud rumbling of thunder jolted us apart. Dhir and I sat up and looked out through the balcony at the rain. It had intensified.

"How is my flight ever going to take off in this?" I cried, as we both ran out to the balcony. It was around four thirty by then, but it was as dark as night. The sky was covered with masses of inky-black clouds and the rain was pouring down as if it was never going to stop. The Great Flood from the Bible must have looked like this, I thought idly, and looked down only to gasp in shock. The entire ground portion of the building was immersed in water at least two feet high. The water was lapping against all the cars parked in the open lot on the side of the building. Luckily, the ground floor had no apartments, only a covered parking lot.

"Shit, my car must be getting swamped in this," Dhir said worriedly. "I've never seen it raining like this. We better call and check on your flight; I'm sure it must have been delayed."

The mobile network seemed to be non-functional, so we tried the landline, which Dhir had to unearth from under a load of old magazines. "No one ever calls me on this," he shrugged, as we tried the airport number.

The electronic voice announced that all flights had been delayed until further notice, due to the inclement weather. Dhir and I exchanged an elated yet worried look. Dhir flipped the TV on and we watched in horrified fascination as the news channels announced that Bombay had been hit by one of the worst ever rainstorms and that all roads were flooded. All forms of transport, from cabs to local trains to flights, had been either cancelled or called off. Clearly, there was no way I was getting out of Bombay that night. I debated whether or not to call Shonali but decided I would get bogged down in all kinds of questions: Where are you? Where will you stay? Come back here only. Blah, blah. By tacit agreement, Dhir and I decided that I would wait out the storm at his flat itself.

We realised we both were starving, having skipped lunch. Clearly, there was no way we could head out in the rain for a meal, nor could we expect any delivery boys, so I had to step up to the challenge. Dhir and I chattered away, as I set about making *daal* and *chawal* while he set the table with the mismatched glasses and melamine plates. He poured out a glass of Sula's Zinfandel, my favourite, and put on some mellow jazz, as I chopped and wept through the onions and garlic. There was a sexual undercurrent that both of us were trying very hard to ignore.

I have to admit, when the meal was ready it smelled pretty good, despite a complete absence of spices (he had none). Dhir had lit two candles and stuck them in the mouths of empty beer bottles. When he switched off the lights, the effect was magical, between the rain outside, the romantic jazz spilling its notes in here and the candle light. Rains are as it is so romantic and when mingled with Dhir's presence . . . I have to confess, I don't remember how anything tasted, whether it was salty or sweet or bitter or tasteless. You could have even fed me fish in there and I probably wouldn't have even noticed (I hate seafood, for the record).

Dhir shooed me off after dinner, offering to clear up and make us Irish coffee. I stood on the balcony and looked out. The apartment was on a service lane beyond which lay the sea. By that time, the service lane had become one with the sea, and only here and there could one see the tips of rocks sticking out. The entire horizon was a deep, deep blue-black, only far away could you see a light here and there, ships out at sea. Not a star was visible in the dark sky, and neither was the moon. The apartment building had only two flats on each floor and they were built at such an angle to each other that each had its complete privacy. The feeling of being on a deserted island intensified as I stood there. Surrounded by the elements, I was loving the isolation of it all.

The rain then changed direction and began beating in at me, drenching me in minutes. I love getting wet in the rain, so I didn't mind. Dhir brought the coffees out and we enjoyed them in rapt silence as we stared out at the sea and the rain, both of us getting soaked. Rahman's brilliance was pounding on the stereo system—*Chaiyya chaiyya, chaiyya chaiyya.* The contrast between the molten hot Irish coffee snaking its way inside us and the cold rivulets of rain water running down our bodies was incredible. Out of the world.

We both set our glasses down at the same time, and, as if synchronised, turned towards each other. There was no hurry, no sense of urgency in the way we came together, only a deep sense of certainty that this was meant to be. Inescapable. Inevitable. Our bodies fused into one another as our lips met for a soul-searing kiss, and the music crescendoed . . . *humma humma humma* . . . Our kisses grew harder and more demanding and our breathing more ragged, and we pulled each other closer and yet closer.

I reached under Dhir's shirt and ran my palms up his smooth back and he literally shivered in excitement. I couldn't bear it any more, I had to feel his hands on my skin. I pulled back from the kiss and peeled off my shirt. Dhir stared at me, as if mesmerised, and then slowly, achingly, put his hands on me. I almost melted away into nothing as he followed it up with tiny little nibbles on my lips.

Dhir then made the most romantic gesture ever—he picked me up and carried me into the bedroom (which, by the way, I hadn't seen so far but which I ended up really liking—white walls and bed linen, wrought iron bed, blue curtains and blue-shuttered windows). We couldn't get enough of each other, and our kisses grew in intensity as at some point we lost the rest of our clothes. The pounding of our heartbeats was so loud that we couldn't even hear the frequent thunder or the rainstorm which was pouring down louder and louder. Dhir looked at me and grew still for a moment, "Are you sure? Absolutely sure?"

"Yes," I whispered.

Dhir moved on top of me and stopped again, "Oh shit! Protection!"

I hadn't even thought about that! Rational thought was, by this time, almost absent from my mind. Thank heavens one of us had some sense left. Dhir sat up and felt around in the bedside drawer. No luck.

"What?"

"Hey, I haven't dated in a while. I don't keep a stash of them handy just in case, you know!"

Could there be a worse *kela*, I wondered, chewing my lower lip as we both stared at each other hungrily (and unhappily). All at once, I yelped and ran out of the room, wrapping the sheet around me as I went. I rummaged around in my bag, grateful that I was a packrat, and my hand closed on a packet and pulled it out. It was the pack of condoms that RKS had handed out at the creative briefing, which then seemed like an event of years ago but was just two weeks in the past. I ran back to find a mystified-looking Dhir and shouted in glee, waving the pack at him, "I've got it!"

"What, you keep a stash around just in case?"

"No, *yaar*, stupid, this is my brief from work."

"Your brief? Or briefs? What does that mean?"

I was giggling, giddily excited as I explained about the campaign and the product samples. Dhir's face relaxed and he laughed, saying, "I hope not all your client's products get a trial run like this."

"Oh, shut up and kiss me."

20

The next three days were pure bliss, except for the seriously uninspiring diet. I did remember to call Mum and tell her I was stuck in Bombay but was fine and staying with a friend, and I had to fib to Shonali that I was staying with a relative somewhere far off. The landline stopped working soon after, so we were anyway cut off from everyone.

We woke up late and showered together. Till the power lasted, we watched lots of movies—he was an AB and Aamir fan like me—and listened to music and sang together. We also rustled up funny meals—scrambled eggs over chips, for instance. We fell asleep at funny times and made love whenever we felt like it. For the first time in my life, I had warm feelings towards my boss—for that pack he had unwittingly tossed in my lap.

After the power went off, we talked—really talked—about all kinds of things and sometimes about nothing at all. I remember reading somewhere that the best relationships are those in which silence is comfortable. Dhir and I, we read in peaceable silence, Dhir his Nelson DeMilles and Stephen

Kings and me the stash of books I had indulged myself in at Oxford and Strand, with our feet crossed over each others. I told him about all the crazy relationships I had been in and he told me about all of his.

On the second day, when we had both gotten seriously sick of the *daal-chawal* diet, Dhir agreed to go to the neighbour's and ask if they had any veggies or fruits left. I would have welcomed beans or even *karela* by the time. I was hoping Dhir returned with some cheese and chocolate.

"Oh, *beta*, you are very lucky you were not in office when the rain began," his portly Gujju neighbour said.

"Yes, Auntie. But I was wondering if I could borrow some vegetables or a fruit or two. I usually have nothing much at home since I rarely cook here."

"Oh, then you must come in and eat with us."

"No, no, Auntie, I'll be fine. Just some carrots or an apple?"

"No, *beta*, this is what neighbours are for. How can I leave you to starve? Come in. Come in, *beta*."

Till now, standing on the threshold of Dhir's flat, invisible to both Dhir and Auntie, I had been laughing heartily at his predicament, but this was nuts—he was having to choose between home-cooked food with the Gujju neighbours and a meal of the sickly *daal chawal* with me! I peeped out from behind the door and made threatening gestures at Dhir, which luckily Auntie wasn't able to see.

"No, Auntie, really, I'm just not hungry right now. I'll come back later."

Auntie must have sensed the note of desperation in his voice. "Wait here," she relented, and disappeared inside her apartment, only to return with a bag of melting frozen peas, a bunch of carrots, some onions as well as some *theplas*, complete with pickle and *dahi*.

"I also don't have too much at home; I was planning to go shopping for vegetables when it started raining that day. I never thought it would turn this bad," she said. "If you need anything else, or you want to come and eat here, you know you're most welcome."

Dhir returned as if coming back home from war. I had by then developed stomach-ache from laughing too hard. Those *theplas* were YUM!

The rain eased up on day three and, by evening, the water had subsided quite a bit. Dhir went out to check his car and returned depressed. "It's trashed. Water has got in everywhere. It's going to cost me a fortune to get it repaired."

The news channels were announcing that flights had been coming and going all day—in fact an incredible 184 flights had landed and taken off that day itself. There was no way I could delay my departure further. I had to leave the next day. It was tearing my heart apart to think of returning to my empty apartment, to a space where there'd be no Dhir to talk with and make love to.

The knowledge that I had to leave soon and that our idyll would end crashed over us like a thunderclap. Neither of us wanted to think about it, but the fact was we didn't know what to do about 'us' once I would be back in Delhi. Was this big enough for us to pull up the stakes, move and start over at our jobs? Could we afford not to take that leap and perhaps regret the road not taken for the rest of our lives?

"Can't you just stay here? Just move here!"

"Dude, I have a job, a flat! My whole life's in Delhi. You move there!"

We stared at each other unhappily. It was too early to have any serious conversations about us and how we were going to make things work out. Anyway, what could we say? It was too early for promises or even expectations about staying together in the long term. While I knew that all the big ad agencies and film makers worked out of Bombay and that my career could head up only if I moved there eventually, I didn't want to make the move out of compulsion, for a guy. If I moved, it must be on my own terms and for the sake of my career. I had just about sobered up on that front and was finally starting to get a little ambitious about my career plans. I had promised myself and Dad that I would take my career seriously. There was no way I could allow romance to sidetrack me at this point. I just couldn't be the ditz who rolls from stone to stone gathering no moss any more. I was the gal who had a plan for her career, for her life, and any guy who wanted me was going to have to deal with it and be willing to meet me halfway and not expect me to move all the way to meet him!

Do you know what it's like to have an elephant in the room that you're trying to ignore? That's what it felt like over the next day as Dhir and I did our stuff, trying to be peppy and all that. Our come-backs had never been snappier, nor our smiles more plastic . . . We made love with a poignant intensity and as I felt his by-now familiar weight on me, I knew I had fallen in love. This was it, the real thing. I felt happy and sad, all at the same time, as I stared up at his face. I didn't want to say the words, though. Nothing freaks a guy out more than a girl who says the three words when he's not ready. And I wasn't sure I was ready to say the words. I mean it's one thing to know what you're feeling but quite another to admit it out aloud.

We were acting like tough dudes at the airport when he dropped me off. Breezy, except for the bone-shatteringly tight hugs we exchanged. I went through the airport process in a daze. I could have gotten on the wrong flight and I wouldn't even have known.

When seated, I opened one of the books I had kept for the flight, Bob Hope's autobiography, *Don't Shoot, It's Only Me.* I had deliberately kept a funny book for the journey but I couldn't even see the words on the page. The letters danced up and down as I was lost in thought.

Dhir :'(

21

Delhi was hot and muggy as usual in this season and I felt begrimed by the time I reached home. The insistent chatter of the cabbie, the loud honking of the traffic had gotten on my nerves, and, with every step, I had felt that Dhir and I were moving farther and farther away, not just physically but emotionally as well. After all, we had only spent—what—four days together. Would that be enough for him to feel something real? Was that enough for me to be certain about my feelings? Had everything in Bombay really happened or was it just something I was blowing out of proportion?

The house felt like a tomb. Dust lay everywhere. Though not Maggie house-proud, I was thankful for something to do. I set about with the broom and the duster and the wiper, madly scrubbing away. Debu turned up at the doorstep just when I had finished.

"Hey, stranger, how was Bombay?"

"Fine."

"Weren't you supposed to get back, like, last week? Dude, were you caught in the rainstorm?"

"Yes."

"So where were you? Were you staying with that girl—Shonali? Was your place flooded? How did you manage?"

"It was fine. I was staying with friends."

"What's the matter, Kaj? You don't sound like yourself?"

"Nothing's the matter. Just stop with the questions and go away. Please, just go away."

"Hey, hey . . . what happened?" Debu came and gave me a gentle hug, eyes kind. "Are you ok?"

Debu's sympathy punctured my balloon of self-sufficiency, and I burst into tears, unable to speak at all, shaking with sobs.

At long last I managed to bring myself back under control and sank down on the sofa. "It's just . . . just . . . I met this guy . . ."

"And? What happened? Did the jackass dump you? You always pick these morons . . ." Debu began heatedly.

"No, it wasn't anything like that at all. It's just . . . Debu . . . Debu . . ."

Debu sucked in his breath, "You've really fallen hard, haven't you?"

I nodded.

"Well then? What's the problem? Is he not interested?"

"No, I . . . he is too."

"So . . . ?"

"I don't know . . . he's there and I'm here. We're three thousand miles apart. How will we ever make this work? It doesn't make any sense."

"What shit! You do know this is the 21st century, right? I mean, you can email and SMS and talk on the phone. Heck, you can always move there!"

"Why does everyone expect me to move? Why can't *he* move? My whole life is here. It's the 21st century and the girl still has to be the one to make all the sacrifices!"

"Whoa, whoa, it's got nothing to do with girl versus boy, kiddo. Sure, he can move if it works for him. Or you can move if it works for you. What's important is making the relationship work, either way."

Debu was right, but I was still hung up on not wanting to move.

"So, anyway, who is this guy?"

"His name is Dhir. He works with an I-Bank in Bombay—the usual IIM, IIT background."

"How did you guys hook up?"

"Actually, we met aeons ago at a wedding in Delhi. It's a funny story but I happened to be hanging out under a table and I bumped into him when I got up."

"What? I never heard anything about it. Tell me about it right now!"

"Don't be stupid, *yaar*. Anyway, it turns out he's a friend of a friend of Shonali's and we all happened to be at Olive for dinner the same night in Bombay, and one thing led to another, and . . ."

"So you, what, dated this guy a couple of times and decided you've fallen for him?"

"Nooo, Debu, you're so dense, *yaar*. No . . . actually . . . we were on a date and got rained in by the storm. We got stuck in his apartment the whole time."

"Oh, I get it. *Roop tera mastana* and all that!"

"Uff, you're really irritating sometimes. I mean, yes, of course I'm wildly attracted to him but . . . it's more than that. We spent a lot of time just talking too, you know, and that too about everything. We could shoot the breeze or talk about the hard, personal stuff with the same ease, and we could just sit in silence together reading our books without feeling alone . . . It's like being at home, you know, a home with an added thrill. We feel the same about so many things, and when we argued it was really stimulating and fun, and we can laugh about the same things . . ."

"You have the dopiest, goofiest, goggle-eyed smile when you're talking about him."

"I do not!" I whipped a cushion off the seat and thrashed Debu with it. But that chat with Debu had done me good. I went to bed with a smile on my face. It was real, what had happened in Bombay.

The next day I hung out with Debu, watching an old cricket match, downing Breezers. I desperately wanted to call Dhir but I was scared to. Scared that he might say "Who?" Scared that he wouldn't say the things I so desperately wanted to hear. Scared that he would say them. Hoping that he'd call me instead. Which he didn't. I went to bed scared, on Sunday, clutching my old teddy who'd been with me since I was four.

On my way to work the next morning, I reached into my bag to call Junaki and tell her to meet me for a latte first at Barista. Great, my phone battery must have run out, the phone was off. I switched it on, hoping it'd have enough battery for one call, only to see a series of messages announcing missed calls and five unread messages from a Bombay number. I prayed hard before opening them. Yes! They were all from him.

I've been trying to call n check that u reached home ok. Missing u, yaar.

30th July, 10.15 p.m.

Going to bed nw. Feeling lonely here widout u. Call me.

31st July, 1.54 a.m.

Hope you've reached home ok. Worried. Been trying to call since yesterday.

31st July, 10.08 a.m.

What's the matter? Hope you're fine. Miss you.

31st July, 1.33 p.m.

Really worried now. Plz call.

31st July, 8.46 p.m.

And there was a message from Shonali too.

'Hey bozo, wat gives? Dint knw u knew dhir all dat well. He calld 2 chk if u'd gotten bck 2 Dlhi ok? Hve u? N is there smthng u're nt telling me?'

31st July, 9.34 p.m.

22

Shit, I had switched the phone off before the flight left Bombay and had forgotten to turn it back on all weekend. Crazy me. Poor Dhir, he must be frantic! I would have loved to call and chat with Dhir right then but didn't want to do it from a public place. I SMS-ed him immediately,

Sorry! Forgot two switch phone on all weekend. All well. Missing you loads. Talk tonight? XXX (I hate abbreviated SMS text).

After the SMS went, I felt a bit hesitant about the XXX, but what the heck, we'd exchanged a lot more than that back at his apartment.

"*Haanji*, madam, using cellphone while driving?" A cop had come up to my window, unnoticed by me.

"Oh, sorry, sir, urgent message."

"Madam, *urgent wurgent kuch nahin hota, challan katega* (Madam, you'll have to pay a fine)."

On a normal day, I would have begged and pleaded and whined my way out of the *challan*, but at that moment I just felt too good. Only one faint problem was nagging me—what to tell Supersleuth Shonali, who has an amazing way of sniffing romances even before the affected parties.

I managed to get through to Junaki who had been enjoying an impromptu holiday since I was AWOL. We met up at the parking lot and sneaked off to the Barista round the corner.

"So how was Bombay?"

"It was fine, good fun to get away from office, actually." I realised it was going to be hard to keep a straight expression on my face when I really wanted to get up and jig around after getting Dhir's message. But I had to try, so I launched into work instead.

"Listen, I've got a great idea for the campaign."

"What?"

"Why don't we think about targeting women? I mean they are the ones most affected, right? We could really have some fun with this and make it an all-women's brand—not sissy or anything but really sexy. Sushmita Sen type of brand, you know."

"But that's so *way* off-base. I mean all the other brands are targeting men. Would women really go for it? Even men are still embarrassed to pick up condoms, women would never do it."

"What if we look at an alternate distribution method? We could distribute this only through beauty salons. That way it's not public and that's a space where you find only female-serving staff. I thought the brand name Lucky sounds good—what do you think? Quite tongue-in-cheek. And we could do a cool campaign about it too—'You never know when you'll get lucky'? What do you think?"

Junaki and I had very different approaches towards work: she was more methodical—dotting the i's and crossing the t's-whereas I typically came up with the wild and way-out-there ideas. But it worked well as a partnership, because it meant we got a mix of the creative and the pragmatic.

She thought the idea over for a while as I silently sipped my latte. She needed some quiet time—to take it in and think through it—whenever I bounced an idea off her.

"Okay, so you're saying this is an urban brand, right? Because there's no way this campaign would work in rural India."

"Yeah, like a brand of condoms called Lucky is really going to work in rural India. I think we should think about different ways to promote this. I mean, no way this ad can go on TV. Maybe we can do an in-film placement? And the Net, of course. We could do magazine ads too. And there are women's credit cards as well."

"Ooh, and we could get some kind of government tie-up on this too since it targets women. We could speak to the welfare ministry or something."

The idea just snowballed from there. The rest of the day was chaotic as we tried to pull all our thoughts together and work out the campaign. We used the tagline I had proposed at Barista, "You never know when you'll get lucky", and had a red colour scheme for the ads and posters—Valentine's Day red. We were wired from the excitement of having cracked the idea and I had a hard time convincing Junaki that I didn't want to go out for a drink afterwards.

I was eager to get home and call Dhir. A bubble of laughter

fizzed inside me as I thought about what our conversation would be like. I had to tell him about the campaign; after all, he had inspired me! I called him as soon as I got home.

"Dhir! I'm so, so sorry about the cellphone. I really am. I was just feeling so bombed when I left that I totally forgot to switch it back on."

"That's ok but . . ."

His voice was stiff and formal. What's up, I wondered, and then the penny dropped. "At work?"

"Yes."

"Ok, call me when you're done."

23

Debu dropped in with a bottle of lukewarm beer, which we had to share since I had run out of Breezers, and we ordered in a pizza. I had to go shopping asap; I was craving fruit and veggies after my four days of insipid diet in Bombay!

"So, did loverboy call you?"

"Shut up, don't call him that. And omigod, I forgot to tell you. I'm such a moron, I forgot to switch my phone on all weekend, and he'd been calling and calling . . ."

"Good grief, a cellphone is just wasted on some people. So did you call him back?"

"Yes, but he's at work. We'll talk later. Only thing is, he called Shonali to check if she knew where I was and now I have to come up with some excuse to keep her blabbermouth shut or this'll be on the front page by tomorrow."

"Shonali, huh? She's a smart cookie, can't keep much from her." Debu had a weird expression on his face. What was that about?

"Yeah, she's such a gossip hound. And she's better than a bloodhound at sniffing out romances."

"Will you stop with the dog analogy? She's quite a nice person."

Okaay, what was going on here? I peeped at Debu and found he wasn't making eye contact, all of a sudden.

"Debu! You have a crush on her!"

"I do not."

"Yes, you do, I can tell. Wow, this is great, two of my closest friends . . ."

"Shut up. There's nothing going on and there never has been."

"But do you want something to happen between you two?"

"No . . ." That was pretty unconvincing. Clearly Debu had the hots for Shonali and I was already dying to do something to get the two together.

"Wait, you will not tell her anything or even give hints. We're not in school anymore. Just let it be, all right?"

"What? Why on earth? I'm not saying she's the love of your life, but you could try dating?"

"Oh really? She's in Bombay, I'm here. She gets paid truckloads of money (that was true, she did!), and I eke out a miserable living as a journalist. Where's the common ground?"

"I'm the common ground. I know both of you. Yes, she earns a lot but she's not about the money, she's real. But, yeah, Bombay could be the deal-breaker. You and Dhir should just exchange places, you know, or we should fall for each other and let Shonali and Dhir date!" (Ouch! It hurt to even theoretically say that and I wished I hadn't.)

Debu started laughing so hard he spilt his beer all over

himself. "Hahaha, us? Fall for each other? Hee hee hee!" It was a little insulting how funny he found it.

"Look, I love you and all, but there's no way I'm falling for you. Never. Okay? You're like . . . you're like the brother I never had, man!"

"Yes, yes, very funny," I said sarcastically. "But that still doesn't sort out your problem."

"It's not a problem, dude. I've met her just once. We barely know each other. I just think she's interesting. And hot. It's not Romeo and Juliet, okay?"

"Fine," I glared and got up to answer the door. The Domino's guy had come.

Five minutes later, I was back to Debu. The pizza in my hand smelt awesome and I was salivating. We polished off the slices quickly and then Debu left, claiming he had work to do. I settled down to watch *Frasier,* my favourite sitcom (after *F.R.I.E.N.D.S.*, I confess). I kept an ear out for my cell to ring, dying to speak to Dhir. It was soon eleven and I was struggling to keep my eyes open in front of the TV and yet Dhir hadn't called.

What to do?

Could I call him again?

Maybe just an SMS.

Waited for your call. Going to bed now, but call when you are free. Really want to talk.

He hadn't called by the next morning, and now it was my turn to get worried. I switched on the TV and found that it had been raining maniacally in Bombay since Sunday. I hoped the same thing hadn't happened all over again, this time leaving

Dhir stranded alone. I had read horror stories already about what people had gone through the previous week in Bombay.

I decided to call him again.

"Yes?"

"Dhir? How are you? I've been so worried after you didn't call last night. Are you ok? I hope you aren't stuck somewhere because of the rain?"

"No, I'm fine."

"Oh, ok. You must have finished work really late last night." I tried to keep an accusatory or possessive note out of my voice, but I don't know how successful I was.

"No, not really. We wound up around nine and then Anoushka suggested we go out for a drink."

"Oh. That's nice. And . . . Anoushka is?"

"She's a friend of mine from work. Anyway, I've got to go now, getting late. See you."

I put the phone down slowly, puzzled and more than a little scared. Who was this Anoushka, now? And why had Dhir sounded so distant, so different? I had always known this long distance thing was all shit! I should never have gotten involved with anyone who lived in a different city! And what did we have anyway? Just a handful of days together. Four, to be exact. And those too under what are called 'test conditions': no work, no friends and no family to intrude upon us. I felt a chill shiver down my spine.

I made my way to office in a daze. With my new resolve, to not let personal stuff impact my work, I managed to remain peppy all day. The campaign was going well. We had come up with product placement ideas for the afternoon soaps, movies and so on. We had to present the campaign to RKS the next day and wanted to make sure we had covered all the bases.

I heaved myself home at about nine, exhausted after the long day at work, the long drive back home and not to mention the heartbreaking phone call with Dhir. It had nagged me all day. I mean, what the fuck was that about? Should I call him back and call him on it? But wouldn't it make me sound pushy? We hadn't exactly made any commitments to each other. He hadn't said I love you. Had the whole thing just been one of those holiday romances—fun but ephemeral? To make matters worse, Debu wasn't around just when I needed his advice. I made some Maggi (God, I really needed to go buy veggies) and gulped it down without tasting it. I couldn't concentrate on anything and rambled around indecisively. It had started raining outside, and the smell and sight of the rain reminded me of those beautiful four days in Bombay. Had that been just last week? It felt like a lifetime ago.

24

My phone rang and my heart leapt at the sight of a Bombay phone number. But, sigh, it was Shonali. I couldn't avoid her forever, so I picked it up.

"Hi," I said listlessly.

"*Hi ki bacchi*, wassup with you? Where were you last week during the rain? Why didn't you return my message, moron?"

"Oh, that . . ."

"Yes that. You better fess up or else." I knew I had to come clean.

"I was . . . well, the day I was supposed to leave I had a date with, uh, Dhir . . ."

"Dhir? WHAAT? You guys hooked up? But you hardly knew him, right?"

"Ye-es, but we'd kind of bumped into each other way back, here in Delhi, and I guess there was something there. When we met up in Bombay it was too much of a coincidence to pass up. So, anyway, the night I told you I was meeting up with college friends?—that was me and Dhir."

"What? You sneaky thing! But seriously, darling, why all the sneaking around? I'm not your mom, you know."

"I know, I know, but I . . . I just didn't feel like talking about it then. So, anyway, we met up the day I was leaving for Delhi. He had taken the day off and we hung out at his place. Then the rain got really bad and I couldn't fly out and so I stayed there till Saturday . . ."

"Oh, what an adventure. So how did it go? Did you guys want to kill each other by the end of it or what?"

"No, that's not it. Actually things went amazingly well. Shonali . . . I think I've really fallen for him . . ." I wailed.

"Heey, that's great, no? He's a lovely guy. Why all this boohooing?"

"I don't know, ever since I came back to Delhi, we just haven't talked. My phone was off on Sunday, then I called him yesterday, but he didn't call back, so I SMS-ed him and then this morning I called him but he sounded so distant, so different . . . maybe he doesn't feel the same way about me, maybe I'm just a ship passing in the night to him . . ."

"Honestly, I don't know him that well. He's just been a part of the gang, so I can't say anything." Shonali said consideringly. "Umm, Ashutosh is a good friend of his and mine too; maybe I could ask him about Dhir . . ."

"Ok, but don't tell him about me, don't tell anyone about me, ok? Just . . . just make up some excuse to ask him. Maybe you can say someone else is interested . . . I'd die if Dhir ever found out."

"Ok, chill. I'll see what I can find out and let you know.

But you'll have to hang on for a couple of days. Ashu's in New York till Thursday."

Debu had come in by then and called out, "Hey, anyone home?"

"Who's that?" Shonali asked.

"Debu."

"Oh. He comes around a lot? Are you sure you don't have something going on with him?"

"What are you, nuts? Of course not. No way!"

"You know what they say—me thinks she doth protest too much."

"What rubbish! But seriously there is nothing going on here. Why, are you interested?"

"Nooo . . ." Shonali said it with less than her usual vigour and I immediately jumped. "Are you interested in my friend Debu here?"

"What 'my friend', you don't own him."

"Yes, but are you?" I teased.

"Well, I don't know. I mean, maybe. But that's beside the point. This is about *you*."

"Wait a minute, munchkin, you can't wriggle out of this. What's maybe interested? Yes or no? Come on, yes or no?"

"Ok, yes, but it's no big deal. I just sorta think he's interesting. We're no Romeo and Juliet, you know."

"Listen, when are you coming here? For work or a vacay, anything?"

"We're supposed to be there for a workshop next week, from Wednesday till Friday; so I was thinking of crashing at your place for the weekend. Why?"

"Just."

"If you set me up with him or breathe a word about this, I swear I will break your bones. I mean it."

"Okayyy!" I trilled as I put down the phone and almost pranced back into the living room. My situation may not have gotten sorted out, but there is nothing I like better than matchmaking. And this one was going to be delicious!

"Whattayou so happy about? Loverboy call?" Debu was parked on the *gaddi*, throwing a steady stream of *masala* peanuts into his mouth. Seriously, sometimes he reminded me of the monkeys in the zoo.

"No, and will you kindly stop calling him loverboy?" Debu had pushed his finger right on the sore spot. I turned the heat back on him.

"Guess who's coming to town next week?"

"I dunno. Loverboy?"

"Oh shut up. I'm not going to tell you if you don't behave and, worse, when that somebody is home, I may not even let you come over."

"Oh man, a fate worse than death. Being without you and your somebody for a whole day would be like . . . like getting Wenger's mango pastry for free."

"You wish. Is that why you're always over here, poaching my food? And, listen, tomorrow can you please pick up some veggies on your way home? My cupboard is literally bare."

"Yeah, yeah, make me do your chores. Ok, fine, but only if you spill the beans right now."

"Ha ha. Very funny. It's Shonali. She's going to be here Wednesday. And only if you're super nice to me will I actually leave you two alone and that too for a whole ten minutes."

"It's going to take a whole lot more than that to make me be that nice to you!"

"Slug!"

"Moron!" But I could tell by his more-than-usually poker face that he was really kicked about the news.

25

The presentation to RKS was due the next morning. Honestly speaking, I was a little nervous—this was the most audacious campaign I had ever done.

"So the campaign thought is that women are the ones most affected by the use or non-use of the condom. Women are the ones to suffer the consequences more. So we've aimed our campaign at women, not men."

"But didn't the brief specifically target men?"

"We've chosen to focus on women to set the brand apart; men could buy the brand as much as women . . . And we can also look at an alternate distribution channel so that it is easier for women to buy them too. For instance, we were thinking of beauty salons, because the staff there is generally all female. Plus, it's also not a public space, so women would have the all the privacy they need to buy the packs."

"Uh huh, uh huh, that's a good thought. But will the company be able to set up this new distribution channel?"

"I checked with the servicing team. Apparently, the company has a line of hair-styling products that they are planning to launch through salons."

"Ok, good. So what's your campaign thought?"

"It's about . . . you know, one of the most frustrating things that can happen when a couple is ready to make out: unavailability of protection with them. Our campaign tackles this head on, and says, 'Because you never know when you'll get lucky!' In fact, we thought the brand name could be 'Lucky'."

He started laughing at that, "That's good, haa haa haa. That's audacious!"

"We thought we could look at in-film placements and maybe in serials too. That might help break the taboo."

The servicing team butted in at this point and we had to take them through the whole thing again. It was funny to watch them as we went through the campaign—their faces turned paler and paler. "What? How can we aim at women? The client asked us to target men."

"But this is too different. The client will never go for it."

RKS stood up. "Look, this is a pitch. Every agency in town will be going the traditional route, targeting men. Either you guys come up with a new proposition or we go with this. At least it's creative, it's out of the box."

"Why not try the 'fun' angle? A campaign where we make the product seem fun?" the Associate Director whispered. He was one of the more conservative souls in advertising, and was finding our campaign and pitch rather embarrassing.

"Oh come on, fun and sex has been done to death since the Kamasutra campaign," I said angrily. "Moods, KS, even Hindustan Latex, have done a sex campaign with their flavoured condoms. Practically, the only brand that hasn't done fun and sex is Nirodh."

"Like I said before, we're going to go with this campaign unless you guys come up with a different proposition. I've gone through all the other campaigns, but none of them have that spark. I'm tired of going for pitches where we put up a whole bunch of campaigns as if we're playing a darts tournament to see which one is closest to the client's dream campaign. I just want to take one campaign for the pitch, and this one it is," RKS dismissed the servicing team. "Ok, girls, I think you've done a fine job. I'd like you to flesh out the scripts a little more. The other thing that I think we could consider is adapting the same thought to a male campaign."

"But . . . but . . ."

"Kajal, I think it's a good thought to target women. At the least, it's unusual. But we have to be realistic too. In India even men don't feel comfortable buying condoms! And we can't just target women, who are going to be even more uncomfortable. If we want to show the client that we are not just creative but that we also have our feet on the ground, then we need to cover all our bases. Ok?"

Junaki and I had never expected a walkover anyway, so this was ok. Actually, it was great: we had kind of won!

We burned a lot of midnight oil in the next couple of days, getting the campaigns ready. RKS also wanted us to work the campaign out in Hindi and that took a lot of doing, because it's quite difficult to translate a line from English to another language or vice versa without losing some of its flavour.

I was getting home so late and so pooped that I had no time to worry about the Dhir situation, which was just as well, because nothing *was* happening on that front. I hadn't heard from either him or Shonali, and whenever I paused long enough to think about it all, I would just feel myself sinking into the Slough of Despond.

I didn't have the guts, frankly speaking, to call Dhir and have it out with him. What if he acted as if he didn't know what I was talking about? In many ways, I was making a monster out of him, because of my own insecurities. Shonali's sodding friend Ashu had extended his stay in NY and was to be back only by Monday. I was thankful to have so much work to occupy me. I had to finish a blindingly boring leaflet about a new car—honestly, why not give this account to a guy who would really appreciate it!—there were endless changes in a small 40 cc black-and-white campaign for an inverter brand and we had to also come up with a new bubble gum TVC for Mishra*ji*.

There he went again, down the same old garden path. "*Kyon na ispe chori chhod dein*?"

"Mr Mishra, *yeh to bacchon ki* ad *hai. Isme toh* adventure *ka* theme *hai* (This is an ad for children, with the theme of adventure). Where will the girl fit in?"

"Pack shot *mein daal dijiye* (Put her in the pack shot)."

"Mishra*ji*!"

"*Accha, meydam, maine ek ad sochi hai* (Ok, madam, I have thought of an ad) . . ."

It's a tough life.

26

Monday was the day of the final pitch presentation. The servicing team was still dithering over my campaign—not whether to present it—that had been decided—but on whether or not to let Junaki and me present it. They were apprehensive that the client might get embarrassed with a woman presenting a condom campaign. Finally, RKS put his foot down.

"Look, it's their campaign, they should present it. If the client was so shy, he wouldn't be manufacturing the product, no?"

Junaki was quite sure she didn't want to talk about the campaign in front of everyone, so that left me.

"Good luck, Kajal, this is a really large account. Do a good job!" RKS said as we filed into the conference room. The client team had a *gora* from the MNC who worked in the NY head office and a couple of desi management types. Servicing went on and on about this research and that one, statistics and numbers, until the client had almost nodded off to sleep. Thanks a bunch, I thought, I'd get the job of waking up the sleeping dead when they'd finally hand off to me!

"To put it in a nutshell, men in India are embarrassed to buy or use condoms. So where does that leave the poor women? Frustrated or at risk. And that's why we propose to aim our campaign at women. They have a right to sexual gratification, as much as men do. And our brand gives them a way to achieve it safely and at their will."

That made the client sit up and take notice. After that, I was on fire. As I went through the presentation of the campaign, I knew without any need for confirmation from anyone else that I had made possibly one of the best presentations of my life. And not only that, it was one of the best presentations the client would see, I was sure of that.

When I finished and sat down, there was a moment of silence and then the client team excitedly burst into animated chatter, asking dozens of questions, exclaiming, nodding in agreement. I was sure in my heart of hearts that we had won the account. This was the first account for which Junaki and I had been the only creative team fronted. And if we had won it, it was going to be a huge leap for me.

The client congratulated us on 'a cracker of a campaign', as the American guy said, and when they left, we were all on a high. I felt a huge sense of confidence and victory flooding me, and in that moment I took a snap decision. It was now or never. I had to get to the bottom of Dhir's behaviour, and I was going to take the bull by the horns. Anything was better than the slow death I was dying by not doing anything.

I got away from the cheering crowd in the conference room, locked myself into our cabin and quickly dialled his number.

"Dhir, this is me, Kajal."

"Yes, yes . . ." there came that cold, distant note again. But I had to plunge in before I could lose my nerve again.

"Dhir, I really need to talk to you. I don't know what's gone wrong but clearly something has. When we were together in Bombay . . . I don't know . . . they were the best four days of my life. Then . . . I'm not sure what happened. Me not switching on my phone, then us not being able to talk . . . you haven't called me back after I called you at office last week. Look, if . . . if you're not interested, if you think what happened in Bombay was just one of those things . . . it's okay. I won't fall apart or anything but I just need to hear it from you. I really thought what we had, what had begun was something special, but . . ."

I plonked myself on the floor cushion and leaned back against the wall of the cabin. I had run out of words and now needed to hear him.

His voice was softer when he spoke at long last. In fact, he almost whispered into the phone, I guess because he was at work.

"I think . . . I thought we had something special too. It was . . . I've never felt that way before. About anybody. I've never felt so close to anyone else."

"Then . . . then . . . what happened?" I was close to tears. Something really beautiful had come into my life and had gone away as quickly as it had come, even before I had fully understood or appreciated it.

"You know what happened."

"Dhir, if I knew, would I be calling you? Come on. Spit it out."

"I spoke to your boyfriend, that's all."

"What boyfriend?"

"The one who picked up your phone when I called."

"What? When? I don't have a boyfriend, Dhir, please! This is stupid. If I were playing games, I wouldn't be calling you."

"Monday night. I called, you didn't answer, your boyfriend did. Or some guy."

"Monday night . . . Monday night . . . oh, that must have been Debu."

"Exactly."

"No, not exactly. Debu is my neighbour and a good friend. Nothing more. We hang out together and often have dinner together. But he has the hots for someone else, and even if he didn't . . . eeww, I don't fancy him!"

"Oh . . . I just . . . heard his voice and I assumed . . ."

Suddenly I got mad at him. What the hell did he think of himself? How dare he assume I was playing around?

"Ok, that is the dumbest, dumbest thing I have ever heard. How dare you assume I was playing around? And to act so childish about it that you don't even answer my calls. You didn't even have the balls to check it out with me, you just jumped to the nastiest conclusion you could. That really hurts. Obviously, all the time we spent together didn't tell you anything about me!"

I banged the phone down and stormed back to the conference room where the celebration was still on. RKS swept us off to the nearby bar—our usual haunt—and we partied good and proper there. If we could have gotten the client to the party too, it would have been a cherry on the cake, but I guess the presentation was good enough. When we reached the bar, I checked my phone to see various missed calls from Dhir, but I wasn't in a mood to answer them at the time. I was still fuming.

I called Debu.

"Hey!" he answered the call.

"What 'hey', idiot! Quickly tell me, did you receive someone's call on my phone on Monday night?"

"Oh, yes! Someone called when you were paying the pizza-delivery guy. It was an unknown number. I said, 'Hello!' But nobody spoke and the call got disconnected."

"Moron! Why didn't you tell me about it?"

"*Arey*, I thought . . ."

"Shut up! Do you know who it was?"

"Who? Oh! Was it Dhir? Shit! I am sorry . . ."

I disconnected the call. It was time to get drunk.

We left the bar hours later, with me truly blitzed by tequila shots. The guys had insisted I take a cab home and I was glad of it, since I was fading out by the time I reached home. I kept remembering my chat with Dhir, now that he had stopped calling me, and I thought, okay, now I have truly fucked it up. I've called him names, ranted at him and not taken his calls for hours. There was no way he was going to go through all that and still want to even talk to me the next day. I was still a little pissed at what he'd assumed. But then I thought he must have been as shaken up by the feelings we had stirred up together as I had been and also as uncertain about how to take things forward. Mum had always said my temper would be the death of me someday. She was right—my temper would certainly cause me a lot of pain some day, if not death. And it looked like that day had come.

I wearily paid the cab and went up. The tequila helped me sleep but my dreams were troubled and I woke up next morning tired and with a headache. I had to take a cab to the office as well and reached in a thoroughly grumpy mood. Even the news that the client had called and asked for a second meeting the same day didn't help me feel any better. It was Junaki's birthday, so we had to go out for the mandatory lunch. We came back to find a huge bouquet, probably from her latest admirer, taking up all the table room in our cabin. "Here," I thrust it at her and slumped at the table, burying my head in my arms.

"But this is for you!" she cried.

"What? It isn't my birthday," I said as I took the bouquet (more like a young forest) from her and pulled out the card. It was from Dhir!

Sorry, sorry, looks like we both have quick tempers. Good match or what? Please call/SMS. Please.

Yes! Game on!

27

I called him immediately.

"Hi!"

"Hi!"

"Apology accepted. And I'm sorry for not taking your calls yesterday and everything."

"It's ok. Free tonight for a phone date?"

"Yes. Nine o'clock?"

"Done."

I heaved a heartfelt sigh of relief. All the tension of the past week and the previous day drained away instantly. At last I had a real smile on my face.

"Who's that?" Junaki asked.

"Just someone. You'll meet him by and by."

The client meeting in the afternoon was . . . interesting.

"We were really impressed by the campaign and the creative approach taken by the agency. We thought it was very, very innovative. But we think it's a little advanced for the Indian market, so we're still thinking about it."

Uh oh . . . where have I heard that before?

"However, we've decided that we would like to go with the agency for the Indian market. And what we'd really like is for you to work with our London office and adapt the campaign for the UK market."

Whoa, hang on there. That's new.

"Excuse me?"

"We feel this campaign has a totally new approach which would work well in the UK and some other countries in Europe as well. So we'd like to start by adapting it for the UK first and then take it from there. We'll send you a written brief based on our research by the end of the week and we'd like you to get started on it immediately after that."

Well, that was one for the books! No one had ever heard of something like this happening before. All of us were totally, absolutely psyched with the news and the new account, and Junaki and I were literally feted by the whole office. Not to mention that I had a chat with loverboy to look forward to.

Could things get any better?

I mercilessly threw Debu out at nine. I did not want yet another messed-up call and I was sure as heck I couldn't have spoken freely to Dhir with Debu hanging around, ready to tease.

"Hi, Kajal!"

"Hey!"

"Listen, I'm really sorry about the way I acted last week, jumping to conclusions. It was really dumb."

"I'm sorry I yelled at you yesterday."

"I'm sorry I . . . ok, wait, is our whole relationship going to be based on apologies? We both goofed up, it's ok, and it's over. Thanks for calling me on it. If you hadn't, we wouldn't be talking right now. And . . . umm . . . I really missed you . . ."

"I missed you too."

"So, anyway, what have you been up to? How's work?"

"Work's good—it's great, actually. We just pitched for this new account and we got it. Not only that, but the client wants to take it international too. And it's all thanks to you."

"Thanks to me?"

"Yeah. Remember our first . . . you know, when you didn't have protection and I had this pack of samples? Well, that was the client we were pitching for. I came up with this totally crazy idea about targeting women and talking about how they should make sure they have protection on hand, just in case they get lucky . . ."

Dhir started giggling and then laughing on the other side.

"Well, it worked and the client loved it. Anyway, how're you? How's work and everything?"

"Ok. I might have to go to Hong Kong for a few days at the end of the week. We have a deal to tie up there."

"Any plans to visit Delhi?"

"I would love to, I really would," his voice dropped an octave to this deep, sensual bass that began to do crazy things to my system, "but this weekend is fraught with work. I'll try and come the weekend after this if it works for you?"

"Yeah, that works." (Heck, I'd make sure it worked!)

"Kajal . . ." his voice became lower and deeper and did strange things to the pit of my stomach. "I really miss you. I hope this doesn't psych you but . . . I've never felt this way before. I keep expecting to find you here when I get home from work and the house feels so . . . empty."

I heaved a deep sigh.

"Yeah . . . I . . . feel the same way . . ."

"The last week, when we weren't talking? Felt like shit. I drank way too much but it didn't really help."

"Same here."

"So . . . I'll talk to my boss about a transfer tomorrow when I get in to work."

"Great . . ."

"And you?"

"We-ell, I could . . . but it's not a great time to talk about it . . . We just won this mega client . . . the campaign's going to be one of the biggest things I've done . . . once it breaks, I can literally walk into any job I want in Bombay or anywhere else . . . It's a really huge break for me . . ."

"Oh . . . ok . . . so when do you think the campaign will start?"

"It'll take about a few months, maybe three-four. In the West these things take a lot more lead time, and they're planning to break this in the UK first. I may have to go there for a couple of weeks to work with the team there."

"God, Kajal, three-four months before you can even consider moving here?"

"Maybe your transfer will come through before then?"

"Well, I'm not sure. These things take time and, you know, I'll be a dead duck in I-Banking in Delhi . . ."

"Oh shoot . . ." I heaved a despondent sigh.

"Listen, there's no point moping about it. We'll do the best we can. I'll try and visit whenever I can and you come down whenever you can. We'll make this work. Hell, Kajal, last week when I thought this was over, I realised how much I wanted this to work. How important you've become. We'll make this work, ok? We have to!"

"Ok, but it's going to be tough. You know how things are nowadays. Marriages break up faster than a pack of cards. And we're so far off from that, we're just at the beginning of something and we don't even know what that is."

"It's not going to be easy, I know, but what's the option? I don't want to give this up, to break up before we've even been together. Do you?"

"No . . . no . . . it's just . . . we'll have to make the effort to make the effort, if you know what I mean. It's so easy to get caught up in what's in front of you and to not bother about anything that is a little farther away. But I really want to try and make this work."

"That's the spirit. And speaking of making things work . . ."

No one has ever made me feel so completely 'melting-into-a-puddle', even with their touch, as Dhir could make me feel just by the sound of his voice from all those miles away at that moment.

28

I felt I was living a strange kind of double-life during the rest of the week, as I went through the day fiercely focusing on work and through the nights ferociously focusing on Dhir. Our phone bills were going to bankrupt me, I was sure, as our late night sessions stretched longer and longer. The cellphone was becoming my new best friend.

Not for too long, though. Dhir flew off to Hong Kong, and we decided to stick to emails, since neither of us had won any lottery yet.

Meanwhile, Shonali landed up, all agog to hear about Dhir and me. It was nice to hang out with someone who knew Dhir and whom I could pump for details. She had finally managed to catch up with Ashu and had downloaded all the goss on Dhir.

"He's supposed to be a really nice guy, but not the boring sorts, if you know what I mean," Shonali said. "He's had a few girlfriends, but no one serious."

"He's told me about most of his girlfriends. I don't care about them. What I want to know is how he feels about me.

Sho . . . I've never said this about any of the guys I've ever gone out with, but . . . I think I'm in love with him."

"Really? Wow, that must have been some stint in the rain. So . . . what happened in Bombay? Come on, give."

"You're such a gossip *na*, Sho. You're just terrible."

"Ok, you're blushing like a bride. So . . . did you guys do it or what?"

I threw a cushion at her but it bounced off and hit my terracotta planter instead. She was like that, Shonali—lucky bitch! Everything just seemed to bounce off her. My cheeks had turned hotter than a *tandoor*, but I had to brazen it out.

"Of course we did it, you moron, we were shacked up together for days. What do you expect? I'm no Jane Austen."

Now it was her turn to blush, since she hadn't expected me to actually 'fess up. Ha, got her!

"So come on, did you get anything useful out of Ashu or not? Shona, seriously, it's driving me nuts. I mean, he acts like he's totally into me and stuff but we only meet on the phone, you know. How do I know if this is serious for him?"

"Well, you can wait for him to tell you, for one thing," Shonali started teasingly, then quickly turned more serious as I picked up another cushion to chuck at her. "The good news is that he hasn't said anything about you to anyone."

"That's good news?"

"Ya, of course. See, if it was something casual, he would have boasted about it by now or tossed around some banter about it. But since he is keeping it under wraps for a while, till probably he can get it figured out for himself, means it's serious."

"You sure?"

"Ya."

Meanwhile, I had to do something to try and get her and Debu together. Debu had started acting like the original Invisible Man as soon as Shonali had come to stay. I marched over to his place on Friday, only to be greeted by the mournful tones of Saigal playing on Debu's old record player.

"Debu, what's up with you, man? I haven't seen you once this week."

"So says she, after discarding and forgetting me like an old shoe all last week when loverboy was in the offing."

"Debu, I'm sorry about that, but you know how crazy our situation is. We only get to talk late at night and . . . I'm sorry if I hurt you . . ." Then I saw he was grinning and punched him on the shoulder. "You moron!"

"Had you going, didn't I?"

"Stupid. So come up for a drink *na*."

"No, it's okay, you guys carry on."

"Why? You're just going to hang around listening to this dopey Saigal all night! Might as well come and drink with us. Have *khana* also, we're going to order from that Thai place and then go out clubbing later. Junaki and some of my other pals are coming too."

"Sounds too wild for my old bones. You carry on."

"What are you smoking? Seriously, come on . . . Oh! I get it. You're avoiding Shonali. But why on earth? If you have the hots for her, I think you should come over and bring some interesting conversation with yourself."

"No way. With my rep, I'd be lucky if she didn't call the cops on me."

"Debu," I said, looking him in the eye, "look, what happened with you was terrible. But it was ages ago. You've got to get over it and have some faith in people. You can't constantly run away from every girl you're attracted to, you know. That's dumb. And Shonali's really nice and . . .," I stopped, remembering that Shonali had made me promise not to give her away to Debu. "Ok, here's the deal. Either you come over or I'm going to tell her you have the hots for her."

"God, with friends like you . . ."

"Exactly, you don't need me to turn into an enemy. So just come."

Debu and Shonali didn't exactly hit it off that evening. I mean, there was Shonali in her club avatar, all boots and mini skirt and asymmetrical shirt, and there was Debu who, just to be as annoying as he could, had come in a *kurta* that could have used a hot iron (and I was tempted to take one to it while he was in it) and an old, worn-out jeans and *Kohlaps*! I could see from the way Shonali rolled her eyes at Debu that this was not going to go well. Then they started arguing about politics, of all things, and Debu, in keeping with his *jholawallah* attire, supported communism, while Shonali of ye multinational bank was rooting for capitalism. The two bickered all the way to the club. Hmm, a fun evening was in store.

The club, called Bed, was a lounge bar. It had white-linen beds instead of armchairs and it was seriously cool to say things like, "Who wants to go to Bed with me tonight?"

"God, Debu is such a moron. How I could have ever thought he was interesting . . ." Shonali cribbed to me when we were freshening up in the club loo.

"He's perfectly nice. Everyone doesn't have to be a corpo type, *yaar*," I shot back.

"Yes, but would it have killed him to dress up in a nice pair of jeans and a tee? I'm not expecting a tuxedo, but those clothes are *seriously* out. And who supports communism nowadays anyway? I mean, even the commies in China and Russia have turned capitalist, but no . . . he can't admit it's a philosophy that only works in theory. I bet he still believes Subhash Chandra Bose is alive."

"You and your philosophies. Who cares? Just have fun."

Debu corralled me at the bar to exchange compliments in turn. "She's so pigheaded. I mean, she can't conceivably admit that anyone else could have an opposing thought that might be correct."

"Ok, clearly you guys were meant for a starter marriage! Let it go already. Just chill, ok?"

They next started arguing about the music at the club: it is too loud, it is toneless, the lyrics rock, the lyrics suck, blah blah. I was pretty relieved when Shonali announced that she wanted to head home. I offered to go with her but she insisted I carry on and took a cab back.

I took a deep draught of my Singapore Sling, my poison du jour, and started getting into the music. "Dance with me," I grabbed Debu's hand.

"Where's your argumentative friend?"

"I think she got tired of arguing with you, so she went home."

"What? I told you not to drag me here."

"Oh relax. I was kidding. She was just feeling tired. She

works incredibly hard, you know."

The next time I returned from the bar, Debu had peeled off home. I was feeling terribly sorry for starting the whole thing about him and Shonali. He was just too sensitive and it must have hurt. I figured I'd apologise to him the next morning.

29

The rest of us partied till pretty late. It was past two when I got home. Some seriously plaintive wailing was coming out of my music system when I entered. God, I thought, the CD must be scratched. I had to shake my head in disbelief a couple of seconds later when I recognised it as KL Saigal's warbling. All due respect, but seriously, the guy was the king of nasal–he could give Himesh competition! I blearily focused my eyes on the *gaddi* and suddenly snapped back to sobriety when I saw Shonali and Debu sitting together and listening to the music, rum and coke in hand.

"What the heck . . .?"

"Oh, hi."

"Don't 'oh, hi' me. You jokers are holed up here, and there I was, feeling so apologetic that I had ruined both of your evenings. Anyway, I'm bombed so I shall take myself bedwards. Enjoy, children!" I waved a hand at them and went to my room, leaving them to it.

Shonali explained the next day that Debu had come over to apologise for ruining her evening and they had wound up with another argument, about Saigal this time. Then Debu had insisted on making her listen to his Saigal collection.

"That guy could be an insomnia cure all by himself!" she huffed.

"Who, Debu or Saigal?"

"Both of them. Seriously, only a deaf woman can spend any time around Debu; he's so full of opinions. Yammer, yammer, yammer! I mean, his idea of showing a girl a good time is forcing her to listen to either him or funeral music!"

Shonali headed back to Bombay on Sunday and I heaved a sigh of relief. Debu and Shonali's arguments all weekend had driven me mad. I was really looking forward to Dhir's visit the next weekend and was debating whether to head out of town somewhere nice, like Neemrana, or just hang out at home with him. I made sure to schedule a visit to the salon with the full works, including a facial, on Wednesday, so that I didn't break out into zits over the weekend.

I actually stressed myself out cleaning up the apartment and then carefully cluttering it, so it didn't look too manicured. Dhir's coming visit had me tied in knots of both tension and anticipation. To top it off, Debu was acting really strange, too busy to come over all week, citing some major 'breaking story'.

On Saturday morning, I was up bright and early, too excited and nervous to sleep any more. Dhir and I hadn't met for three weeks. I rushed through my bath and dithered over getting ready, first choosing one, then another outfit, and then another. The whole plan was to look casually glam, and I wasn't that good at combining casual with glam.

The doorbell rang when I was almost ready to leave for the airport. I grabbed my bag and rushed to the door, wondering who had turned up so early on a Saturday.

"M . . . mom?!!" My voice turned alarmingly shrill.

"Hi, *beta*, where are you rushing off to so early on a Saturday? Work?"

"Wor . . . ya, ya, yes, work . . . what on earth are . . . I mean, what are *you* doing here?"

Then I noticed the big suitcase at her feet.

"And how long are you here for?" I said weakly.

"*Beta*! I was missing you, and papa is travelling for the next week—ten days—so I thought I would come and visit you. We have hardly spoken to you in the last few weeks. You have been so busy since your trip to Bombay."

"Oh . . . oh, come in, Mom. Come . . ."

Come in. Come in.

Ok, I loved my mom to pieces, but why on earth did she choose to spring up that day? Thankfully, she had popped up before and not after Dhir had landed. But, still, why then? I cast an accusing eye upwards in disgust and then realised I had to do something quickly. I must warn Dhir about this situation asap. I did not want Mom to meet Dhir at that stage and scare him off. She was really sweet and all that, but she had a way of scaring off potential boyfriends either by grilling them to death about their values, future plans and all that jazz, like an overprotective mother hen, or by being so sweet to them that they thought she was picturing them as a potential son-in-law. Which she probably was, by the way. It would have been interesting to see which reaction she would have had to

Dhir, but I didn't want to go through the process of watching Dhir's reaction to her.

As I put her suitcase away, she followed me around, straightening out a (artfully strewn) cushion here and a stack of magazines there, and I racked my brains to think of how to get away for a couple minutes and call Dhir.

"Mamma, want tea?"

"Yes, *beta*, that would be great. But, you sit, I'll make it. I know you miss my chai."

"Oh, I just remembered, I am out of milk. I'll just go borrow some from Debu."

"Who's Debu?"

"My neighbour from downstairs."

"Oh, that sweet boy who looked after you when you were ill? Ask him if he'd also like some *chai*, okay?"

I gave her a tight hug on my way out. Despite the fact that she had scuppered my romantic plans, I was still happy to see her.

At Debu's, I frantically dialled Dhir's number, praying his flight had landed, and that I could speak to him, and not have to leave an SMS instead.

"Dhir, where are you?"

"Just landed. Where are you?"

"Listen, you can't come over to my place. My mom's landed up to stay for a few days."

"What? When? WHY? What am I supposed to do here! I came just to catch up with you."

"I know, I know, and I'm really sorry, but now she's here suddenly and I don't know what to do!"

"Good grief, what am I supposed to do now?"

"Don't you have any friends you can stay with? Or some relatives?"

"Yeah, sure, that's why I came all the way from Bombay for the weekend—to hang out with friends or relatives."

"Dhir, sweetie, I'm really, really sorry but I swear I had no idea she was coming. Seriously, do you have anyone you can stay with? I can get away from the house for a while and we can meet up, only not the way we had planned."

There was a long silence, and then Dhir sighed and said, "Ok, I guess it can't be helped. I'll call a couple of pals and see what I can do. Let me know when you can get out. But you owe me, big time."

"I know. And thanks. And I am sorry."

I went back up feeling all mixed up. Dhir was being really nice about this and I felt a bit guilty about what he was going to have to do, and about being less than ecstatic about Mom's visit.

"Where's the milk?"

"Huh?"

"I thought you went to borrow some milk? And is your friend coming for tea?"

"Oh . . . oh that! I totally forgot about the milk. I'll just get it." I said dreamily.

I rushed back to Debu's, leaving Mom muttering about 'this younger generation' and how we'd forget our heads if they weren't attached.

30

Claiming work, I managed to slink out of the house an hour later. By this time, Mom was all stirred up supervising the maid and ordering groceries to restock my kitchen and organising my wardrobe by colour. Dhir was holed up with a friend of his in Def Col, which was a good one hour away from my yuppieville Gurgaon apartment. So we decided to meet halfway, at the PVR Saket market.

He was squatting by the second hand booksellers, going through their stacks of books, as yummy as ever in a deep blue linen shirt and a light blue pair of jeans. I had to admit I'd begun wondering whether he was really as handsome and sexy as I remembered him from our days in Bombay in those three intervening weeks. But when I saw him then, I realised he looked even better than the image of his that I had been carrying around in my mind . . .

"Hi," I said softly as I came up to him.

His eyes lit up as he stood up and he caught hold of both my hands. "Hi!"

Both of us had manic grins on our faces; we were crazily

happy to see each other. I was dying to hug him, to kiss him, well, actually a whole lot more than that, but Delhi is not exactly the place for PDA. I'd have to wait.

"How long are you out for?"

"Till the evening. I told Mom I had work and stuff." I'd had to do a whole lot of 'covering my tracks' before coming, including SMS-ing Junaki to tell her not to call even by chance. But I still had unrealistic and dreadful visions of bumping into one of my numerous relatives or family friends. Then there was also the possibility that someone from office might call on my landline number. Sneaking around is hard work!

"And tomorrow?"

"No, there's no way I can get out tomorrow. Even Mom knows I never work on Sundays."

"Ok, no sweat. Where can we hang out for now?"

What I really wanted to do was find an intensely private place and . . . What about your friend's place?"

"No good. He's at home sleeping off a major hangover. Plus his landlady is the suspicious type, so he's not allowed to bring women over."

"Oka . . . ay, then let's just head into the Barista here and later we can have lunch at Azzuro? Unless there's something in particular that you want to do in Delhi?"

"Not something, someone. But that's impossible so, yeah, coffee it is."

I grinned up at him and we walked to the Barista, hand in hand. It wasn't quite the way I'd envisaged meeting him again after so long; but it was great anyway. We went through endless cups of coffee as we talked and argued and laughed and later ate our way through Azzuro's amazing mezze and thin-crust pizzas, holding hands under the table.

"What are you going to do through rest of the weekend?" I asked finally.

"Gaurav is probably going to drag me clubbing tonight, and then I'll head out sometime tomorrow afternoon."

"I'm really sorry about this, Dhir. You're being so nice about it."

"Hey, it's ok. Unfortunate timing, but you have to spend time with your mom, and I understand that. We'll have our weekend together some other time."

"Maybe I can come to Bombay next weekend, if Mom has left by then."

"That'd be great. Come on, I'll drop you home now."

We held hands all the way and sat pressed close to each other. Both of us were back in the dumps at not being together the rest of the weekend. Dhir got out of the car and insisted on opening the door for me. This is something which I usually find rather weird (who has the time to wait for the guy to run all the way round the back of the car to the passenger side and then open the door?), but with Dhir it made me feel all fragile, ladylike and cherished. There was nothing ladylike about the bone-shatteringly tight hug we exchanged when parting though. I watched the Indica all the way out of the gate till I couldn't see it any more. My shoulders were slumped and my eyes glazed with tears as I got into the lift. But when I reached outside the apartment, I put on my best smile for Mom.

She'd done wonders with the place while I'd been gone. It now looked as if a real human being lived there. She'd put some flowers in a vase on the dining table, bought a few potted palms from the nursery down the road, and spread a new mirrored bedspread on the *gaddi*. The windows were thrown open and the drapes pulled back to admit fresh air and the yummy fragrance of home made food filled the air.

"*Beta*, what a long day you've had at office, even on Saturday. They make you work so hard," Mom complained as she bustled out of the kitchen with a glass of cold water for me. "Thanks, Mom, but don't work so hard. You've come here for a break, so chill. We can always go out and eat or order in. Or I'll cook," I said guiltily.

"*Beta*, it's not hard work to come and look after you. I enjoy it," Mom said, ruffling my hair. "I don't even know when you became so grown up—living in a city far away from us, all by yourself. I miss taking care of you. Your brother is also so far away."

I felt bad for her—she had spent her whole life taking care of us, had poured herself into the task since the day we were born. And now that we had grown up and become independent, what was she supposed to do? And what were we supposed to do?

"Now it's time for me to look after my grandchildren. But you two are so hopeless. Looks like my time will be up even before I see your wedding, let alone any grandchildren."

She was back on her usual track like a broken record. That cut my sympathy short immediately.

"Look, Mom, I'm not going to get married till I feel like getting married. That's not the only thing people do in life any more. I have a career, I have my friends, I want to travel, see the world, do a whole lot of things. Marriage will happen only when it fits into my plans, and not the other way around."

"You children talk a lot of rubbish these days and you're all so opinionated. My God! We would never have dared to talk back like this to our parents."

"Yes, and just look where it got Charu *Masi*." Charu *Masi* was Mom's younger sister. She'd been in love with someone but my grandparents had fixed up her marriage with someone else. *Masi* hadn't had the guts to tell them 'Thanks, but no thanks'. The guy she'd married had turned out to be a louse besides being an alcoholic abusive MCP. Things got so bad that *Masi* had to eventually run away from home, at the ripe old age of forty-two. We hadn't heard from her since then, and it was one of the unspoken rules of the family to not mention her, even in passing.

My mother was more than taken aback by my remark and turned tearful five seconds later. "When did I say we would force you kids into anything? We have tried so hard to be liberal, to give you all your freedom, to listen to what you want to say . . ."

Mom belonged to the Nirupa Roy School of Motherhood and was a master at evoking guilt. I didn't know if she did it deliberately, but she was always successful at making me feel how far I fell short of being a perfect North Indian sweet, submissive, self-sacrificing daughter. I think I have a little too much testosterone—maybe X and ½ Y, instead of X and X.

"Mo-om, I didn't mean it like that . . . I just . . ." Sigh! "Ok, can I have some tea?"

Asking Mom to do something in the kitchen worked like a

charm. She could forget everything else in her vigour to satisfy our hunger or thirst. After that tearful exchange though, there was no way I could have gone out for dinner and left her alone at home, so I regretfully SMS-ed Dhir. Our hot weekend together was turning out to be a real snooze-fest!

31

Mom stayed through the next weekend as well, and since I lived in a one-bedroom flat, she shared my room, leaving me with no way of talking with Dhir on the phone at night. We could only talk through emails and IM. Mom asked me about work, and I told her in detail about the new campaign, though, of course, carefully omitting the details about how I'd come up with it.

"What? You're going to do a campaign on condoms?"

"Yes, Mom. It's really cool! They're going to launch it in the UK!"

"Oh, only there *na*?"

"No . . . oo, it's going to be launched here too. I've been exchanging emails with our UK branch and they're really excited too. They think it might win a Cannes or something. I'm going to be famous, Mom!"

"Good Lord, for a condom campaign? What will people say? It's outrageous. What's wrong with your boss? Why did he give this thing to a woman? It's demeaning!"

"Mo-om, have you lost it? It would have been demeaning

the other way round, that is if he hadn't given me the opportunity just because I'm a girl. This is a really good break for me."

"I don't know about any of that," she retorted with special motherly logic. "But what I do know is that I won't be able to hold my head up in the community any more. What if anyone finds out you have done this shameless campaign for this . . . for this . . . sleazy product? Everybody will think you are *that* kind of girl. There will be no chance of you ever getting married! Kajal, please, can't you stop the campaign?"

"No, Mom, this is a good thing! And so what if no one wants to marry me because of this? I wouldn't want to marry nerds who think like that anyway! And what is this community business, huh? This is 21st Century India. No one cares what the neighbours think."

"That may be true here, amongst you flighty young people living in Gurgaon, where you don't even know the name or caste of your neighbours. But any normal person living in a normal place does know his or her neighbours and does care what other people think. Can you at least ask them not to print your name in the campaign?"

"Mom, no one's name is going to be printed in the campaign, ok?" I omitted to tell her that press releases about our bagging the account and the campaign's going international had already been sent out by the agency to agencyfaqs and other agencies covering the ad industry. I was hopefully not going to stay anonymous much longer, but why torment her with the truth?

Mom went into panic mode anyway, to the extent of calling Bunty over for dinner. He was the last person I wanted to meet, so I was pretty pissed at this and retaliated by forcing Debu and Junaki to join the merry throng. Debu was still holed up at home, working on his breaking story or whatever. I'd hardly seen him in the last two weeks. Mom had met him briefly and had been really sweet. "After all, you saved my daughter's life!" she had gushingly and melodramatically said after every second sentence during their rendezvous. But she was really annoyed to find him—now a "kebab mein haddi"—in her plans to thrust Bunty and me together.

"Why have you called them here today?" she hissed at me, as I started helping her carry the dishes to the table.

"Because they love *biryani*," I hissed back.

"So we could just have sent some later!"

"Mom, they're my friends."

"Why can't you be friends with Bunty?"

32

Ok, this technique of our parents completely mystifies me: their pushing two kids together and telling them to 'be friends and play nicely together'. Heck, if that approach worked, America would have had Israel and Palestine playing marbles together in a *gali* today. And Bunty and I were way beyond the age when we could keep up the pretence of playing together. At least, I was.

"Bunty, *beta*, you should really keep an eye on Kajal. See, she's living here all alone in this big city."

"Yes, Auntie, and the city is getting worse every day. But what to do, she is so busy, she never has time for me."

My mouth fell open. What in the name of crap was this?

"Mom, I don't need anyone else looking after me. I do fine by myself. And I have friends—Debu and Junaki and Shonali and . . ."

"Yes, *beta*, but people with whom one has grown up are quite different *na*? They have your true wellbeing at heart. Don't you think so, Bunty *beta*? Here, have some more *biryani*." Bunty by then had already eaten a mountain of the stuff.

"Auntie, don't you worry about our Kajal here. She's more than capable of looking after herself. She's a regular Basanti." Debu shoved his oar in.

"Basanti? Who's that? Do I know her?"

"Basanti from *Sholay*, Auntie. The Hema Malini character. Or, on second thought, maybe more like Dhanno?"

"Haha, very funny." I kicked Debu hard on the shin.

"Auntie, you should get her married. She's totally out of control." Debu continued.

I stared at him, horrified. What had come over him? Mom would freak, you moron!

"Out of control? How? What has she been getting up to?"

"Oh nothing, Mom, Debu's just pulling your leg." I glared at Debu, daring him to speak one word more. Wind up Mom and she was liable to park herself with me for the rest of her life or at least till getting me married off to a boy of her choice.

"Bunty, you see, this is why I tell you to watch out for my Kajal. She's such a naïve thing, and boys in Delhi are so spoilt." She didn't want to even tell Bunty about the campaign, she was so embarrassed and mortified by the whole thing and so worried about 'my chances'. I think she was hoping he'd propose to me by the end of dinner and I'd be married and expecting before the week was out.

Bunty smirked and said, "Of course, Auntie. I'll be glad to do it. Kajal, why don't you come out with me and my friends tonight?"

With Mom egging me on, there was no way out. I dragged Junaki along for protection to meet Bunty and his gang of boys at Someplace Else that night. His friends and he were an unintentionally funny group of macho types, whose idea of a good conversation was to compare whose were bigger—biceps, that is.

"I'm sorry, Junaki. Maybe we can *cut-lo* and go off by ourselves in a bit."

"Why? These guys are hilarious. I think Bunty's really sweet. And I totally have my eyes on his friend Miklos!" Junaki had a yen for firangs, and Miklos was this tall, rather good-looking friend of Bunty's from Ukraine.

With that, Junaki was off to the dance floor with the gang of boys, most of whom couldn't dance their way out of a paper bag, but she somehow seemed to be having fun. I saw her maneuvering to dance closer to Miklos from the corner of my eyes, while doing some surreptitious and frantic SMS-flirting with Dhir. The way my life was going, our relationship was poised to end before it even got into second gear. Maybe I should think about the transfer, after all. Maybe.

"Hey, who're you SMS-ing?" Bunty hopped up on the bar stool next to mine.

"None of your business."

"Come on, don't be like that."

"Look, Bunty, we've never been friends, so let's just cut this out, okay?"

"Babes, you've never been friendly. Is that my fault? I even offered to bring you here tonight, out of sheer pity for you and your poor mom."

"What the fish! You're such an asshole. I have a pretty good life. I don't need any help from you. Thank you very much."

There was an awkward pause after this, during which we both watched the others dancing like there was no tomorrow. Especially Miklos and Junaki who were shimmying together by then, both very close to each other.

"Why'd you drag that friend of yours here anyway? She seems like a bit of a flirt!"

"Why should that bother you? You should be only too happy that someone's willing to flirt with you!"

"But she is not flirting with *me*. She seems to have the hots only for Miklos!"

"Jealous much, eh?"

"Nah! Anyway, one dance?"

"Let's go. Dancing would be better than talking with you."

Bunty was a pretty good dancer, I'd have to give him that, and we had a good time on the dance floor, so much so that I forgot to be mad at him. At some stage, though, the dancing turned into a melee and I found myself grooving with Junaki more than Bunty, who himself was busy showing Miklos some bhangra moves. That's when I decided to call it a night and head home.

33

Mom answered the first doorbell the next morning to bring back an oversized bouquet of red roses and carnations. It was from Bunty! The card had this super soppy message: "Please give me a chance!" I don't know whether he was on some dope or not, but he was a dope all right. We'd had fun the previous night, but not even in my wildest dreams had I imagined he'd misunderstand stuff. See, this was why we were not friends. He was not a cool guy.

"*Arrey*, *beta*, see I told you Bunty and you are a great pair. See, what a lovely bouquet he's sent you." In my opinion, it was a hackneyed bouquet; I preferred exotic stuff, like birds of paradise or anthuriums, but that was beside the point.

"Mom, just because he likes me does not mean I like him, okay? We have nothing in common. I only went out with him because you forced me to and that was it. The End."

"*Beta*, how can you decide in just one evening? What you should do is to spend more time with him."

"It's not one evening; I've known him my whole life. He does not push my buttons."

Mom continued to be really pushy about this, and it didn't help matters that Bunty called up and whined his way into a dinner at my place again.

"*Hai*, he's dying to see you! Isn't it exciting?"

Sometimes I think parents and their children speak in a foreign language to each other. Couldn't Mom read my lips? I mean she spent her whole day scurrying around the house, cooking up all kinds of fattening, artery-clogging stuff, completely deaf to my pleas that the only way Bunty could be her son-in-law was if my brother magically changed into a woman, got a lobotomy and then married him.

The disgusting evening was made worse by the fact that Debu had disappeared into thin air and I was left with no buffers. Bunty behaved like a duplicate of mamma's-darling Rocky/Salman Khan from a Sooraj Barjatya movie: all saccharine smiles and soft-voiced compliments. I felt so out of place that I actually contemplated getting into a purple *ghagra choli* and breaking into a song from *Hum Aapke Hain Kaun* to fit in!

The rest of Mom's stay was rendered intolerable by Bunty's crackpot behaviour: bouquets every day (one for me, one for Mom), dropping by for dinner every other day, offering to drop Mom to the station (which she happily accepted much to my dismay), taking Mom shopping and then turning up at office with her in tow to take us both out for dinner.

I rediscovered how little I had in common with Bunty in those days. Most of the conversation over dinner was between Mom and him, and it was all about either neighbours back home or their kids and what they were doing, just reminiscing about the good ol' days in short. I personally hadn't kept in touch with anyone since moving to Delhi for college and felt I was too young to turn nostalgic.

"What's wrong with you? Why have you been acting so weird?" I took Bunty to task the minute Mom's train left.

"What do you mean, 'acting weird'?"

"You know, all the flowers and coming over for dinner and all? I've been living in Delhi for—what—nine years now, and have happily managed without so much as catching sight of you by accident. And now you're all over me like a rash!"

"I . . . I don't understand what you mean, Kajal," Bunty's voice went all soft and quiet. Oh no, he was back in his Salman-Khan-as-Prem mode! "I . . . I've always liked you . . . But you never gave me any hint . . . And then when Auntie came and called me over for dinner, at last, I thought, at last, Kajal is giving me a sign."

"Bunty, have you gone mad?" The New Delhi Railway Station was no place for an argument. Passersby were jostling us from all sides. Some even stopped to stare, but I couldn't care less. "I've never given you any hint or sign! We have nothing in common. If you weren't Mom's best friend's son, I'd have lost track of you after school, and you would have done the same to me, I'm sure."

"Kajal, don't say that. I really thought . . . Kajal, I'm in love with you. Kajal, will you marry me?" And lo behold, in the middle of the New Delhi Railway Station, on a crowded platform, with hundreds of nosy eyes on us and dozens of hands touching us at the rate of two per second per square metre, Bunty the Loon, got onto one knee and produced a ring! I was speechless as he rambled further, "Kajal . . . I've grown up with you. All my life I've dreamed of you. Whenever I saw my future, it was always with you. Please, please, say yes!"

I thought I was in the middle of a Hindi film shooting. This was one of the most romantic proposals I had ever heard, both in real life and in movies and TV. But it was coming from the wrong guy! To make matters worse, the nosy eyes and touchy hands had, by then, gathered in a circle around us, as if we were actors in a *nukkad natak*.

As soon as Bunty finished proposing, calls and cries started emanating from the crowd,

Arre, what a lovely proposal. Lucky girl!

Say yes na, Beta, a motherly type was egging me on.

Haan kar de, guys in the crowd were whistling and saying.

Haan kar do, the girls in the crowd were giggling and whispering.

I couldn't believe what was going on. I shook my head, just to make sure I really was in the middle of this, a movement which the crowd obviously didn't approve of. They then read my face and realised I wasn't going to marry Bunty ever and broke into a loud and prolonged hiss. Then boos and jeers started, as I slowly backed away from Bunty. By then, I was beginning to get a little scared of the crowd and their reaction, but then I couldn't lie to Bunty either. I took his sweaty hand in mine (see, that's another reason I had never had the hots for him—his hands were slimily wet all the time, even in winter!) and said, "Bunty, you're . . . I'm really, really shocked. I'd never thought you felt this way about me . . . But,

Bunty . . . you're like a brother to me . . . I've never thought of you as anything else." (Okay, so I didn't really think of him as a brother, or rather I didn't think of him at all, but I couldn't say *that* with the mob watching me with violence in their hearts, could I?) ". . . I'm really sorry that I'm hurting you like this . . . If anything I said or did convinced you otherwise, I'm really sorry, but . . ."

Bunty stayed on the ground and his face went pale. He bowed his head down and the crowd's comments started to get really nasty.

Aisi ladkiyon se to door hi rehna chahiye.

Pata nahi kya samajhti hai apne aap ko.

Dekhte hain kaise haan nahin karti!

Spotting a small break in the circle of louts around us, I ran all the way out of the station, and fell into an auto, asking the driver to take me to CP. I actually held my breath till the auto got out of the station, half expecting the mob to come after me. What a nightmare!

That evening, as soon as I reached home, I wanted to call Dhir but then I remembered his crazy reaction to Debu and figured it could wait. Dhir and I really had to get our act together. I was missing him with an intensity that grew with every single day. Every day, I couldn't wait for it to be nine o'clock so that I could call him and talk to him. The past ten days had been tough on both of us.

Then I thought, harking back to Bunty's proposal, that if that had been Dhir back there . . . and I started giggling. Some things look and sound romantic in movies, but I knew if Dhir had gotten on his knees and proposed in the middle of the station, on a platform with *paan* stains all over, I would have probably burst out laughing.

But then I would have also said yes to it all.

34

After a while, Dhir and I started to feel bogged down by mere phone romance. We couldn't remain hermits forever, so we went out and partied with friends on weekends as usual. On weekdays, work sometimes got so hectic for both of us that we would decide to 'talk to you tomorrow'. Moreover, Dhir had begun to travel quite a bit such that our time zones often didn't match. Within a month, I had maxed out my credit card and had no money to travel. Dhir barely managed to visit me one weekend after two months of trying. Despite all this, things were always great whenever we met up or chatted or talked on the phone.

But slowly it started being not enough any more. There were so many times when I just wanted my boyfriend with me, right next to me, at a party, or when I was watching a movie or even just pottering around the house . . . and I guess it was the same with him. I wanted to be able to see him whenever I felt like and not to have to juggle the whole Delhi-Bombay-money-time-work thing. I just wanted to have a normal life and not to be rushing around the whole time managing friends, work,

Dhir, parents, make-up and home. I wanted a real hug, not an emoticon.

Debu was finally back from his mysterious trip, so I headed over to his flat to have some company in my misery.

"Where have you been? You didn't even tell me before you left!"

"Oh, I was in Bangalore . . . to report on this big story."

"What big story?"

"Oh, er, this big . . . political thing that's been brewing there. Forget it, you wouldn't be interested."

"Okaay . . . but aren't you a travel writer?"

"Is there some kind of rule that you can never change or do or be anything else than what you do or are?" he said, rather aggressively.

"Chill, moron, of course you can! You know I . . . missed having you around. And I've got so much to tell you!" I filled him on what had been happening—or rather, not happening—on the me-and-Dhir front.

"Seriously, Debu, what should I do?"

"Hey, I told you on day one—move to Bombay."

"Come on, be serious. I can't just up stakes and move."

"Why not? What are the stakes anyway? You can probably get a transfer or find another job in Bombay. You're now well known in advertising with all the PR about your campaign. What's the problem?"

"It sounds too needy, too desperate. And what if it doesn't work out after all these changes, these compromises I make to be with him?"

"What's needy or desperate about it? You're trying to make

a relationship work. If you really think it's worth a shot, you should do it. Don't worry about your career, you'll do fine. But special relationships don't come along every day. And so what if it doesn't work out? Isn't finding that out worth the price of moving? Look, what you want from the deal is a guarantee, and life doesn't come with any guarantees. Sometimes you just have to put yourself out there and see what happens. If it doesn't work out, it doesn't—you learn something and move on. And then at least you are not tormented by thoughts of the what-ifs and what-it-might-have-beens," he said forcefully.

After a silence of a minute, I called up Shonali to ask what she thought about it. She had become a little closer to Dhir lately, thanks to our romance.

"Look, he's a great guy, and I think he's really into you. But I don't know. I wouldn't make a move like this. It's too scary. But that's just me."

"Thanks, you're a great help," I hung up and turned back to Debu. "Now I'm even more confused."

"Babes, you have to figure out what's right for you on your own. No one else can help you do that!" He went off looking like Devdas and I nursed my rum and coke like Chhoti Bahu from *Sahib Bibi aur Ghulam*.

That night when Dhir called, he sounded different, quieter.

"Kajal, this distance thing is really getting me down. Sometimes I feel as if we're not really in a relationship and that it's just a figment of my imagination."

"I go through that too. It's really crazy, Dhir. Do you think we're crazy to try and make this work? There must be easier relationships."

"I guess . . ."

"So when can you come down next? It's been ages . . ."

"Look, Kajal, what I was wondering is . . . Look, are you going to be able to move to Bombay anytime soon?"

"Dhir, I told you it's not possible right now. I have the UK campaign and everything coming up. In fact, I'm going to be in London for two weeks, starting end of next week. What about you? I thought you were trying for a transfer?"

"I have talked to my boss about it, but so far it hasn't worked out . . . Can't you just move here and we'll take it from there?"

"No, why can't you move here and we take it from there? Why should I give up my job at this stage?"

"No, no, that's not what I meant, I'm just . . . feeling frustrated . . ."

"If you find our relationship so frustrating, maybe we should call it a day . . ."

"Please, K, don't fly off the handle. That's not what I meant. Shit, it's really getting tough. Isn't it?"

"Dhir . . ."

"K . . . I think . . . I'm going to hate myself for saying this but . . . if neither of us can move . . . then what are we doing? We're just opening ourselves to more pain when we do eventually break-up . . ."

I took a long moment to pause and think. The comforting castles that we had built up between the two of us were only based on a handful of days actually spent in close proximity. Was that enough for either of us to toss our hearts over the fence and take a blind leap of faith? At that point of time,

I was unsure about it all. We were still relatively new in our careers. We had a lot of work to do to stand firmly on our feet. We couldn't afford to be quixotic about stuff.

"I . . . I agree . . ." I could hardly speak, my voice was so choked.

"K . . . this is crazy . . . I feel like I'm losing my best friend . . ."

"Me too . . . Dhir, I . . . I can't talk any more. Take care . . ." I hung up and switched off my phone. I didn't want to talk any more, to hear either his voice or that of reason in my head. I wanted to curl up into a little ball and disappear . . . I didn't want to talk to anyone, to see anyone . . . I just lay there in the darkness all night, almost bereft of thought, hugging my old teddy to myself. He'd been through everything with me . . . he was with me in this too . . .

Debu thought we'd both lost our minds.

"So, to avoid the pain of a break-up, let's break up? Are you guys off your rockers or something? I just don't get it. You guys are so good together!"

"How do you know? You've never seen us together."

"I don't have to. I've seen your face when you talk to him. I've seen you the last couple of months, the way you're so lit up from inside all the time. I'm telling you, this is a stupid, stupid move. Even for you!"

I didn't want to hear any more about it. I could still hear a phantom shriek of pain whenever I thought about it. I didn't even have a picture of Dhir, I realised. In five years or three or two, would I even remember what he looked like? He had touched a chord in me that no one else ever had. And, yet, he could fade out of my life as if he had never been there. Only my heart would know . . . I wished I could recall the phone call, turn back the clock, so we'd still be together. But he was right. If he hadn't said it that day, I would have said it. This was one of our weird things—we often completed each other's thoughts, each other's sentences . . .

Ok, I must stop thinking about him and start working on the campaign. This was the first time I was going abroad, that too on work. I had to let him go to concentrate on my career and it would all be in vain now if I didn't focus on work.

Two days before my flight, I took a leave and surprised my parents with a visit.

"What's the matter, *beta*? You look terrible!"

"Thanks, Mom, you always know how to make your girl feel good."

"You're going for that embarrassing campaign of yours, aren't you? I don't know what to tell the neighbours, *haye Bhagwan*!" God! We were still on that?

Dad was a little more encouraging, "Ignore her, she doesn't know what she's saying. Our little daughter is going off to teach advertising to the *goras*. That's something to be proud of."

Neera Auntie, Bunty's mom, dropped by to give Mom her *katori* back. She would borrow some kitchen stuff or the other from Mom every single day, without fail. She acted kind of cold when she met me.

"What's up with her?" I asked Mom.

"*Beta*, I don't want to bring this up now, what with you going off to London and all, but poor Bunty! *Tumne accha nahin kiya uske saath* (You didn't treat him well)."

"WHAT? Mamma, I don't like him. I had no idea he felt that way about me. Eek! I can't marry someone just so that I don't hurt their feelings, no?"

"Haan, *beta*, but think about it: he is a good boy, from a good family and they are our close friends. Everyone would be so happy . . ."

"No, not everyone. Me, for example?"

"Then why are you looking so pulled down? I thought maybe you have reconsidered, maybe you are regretting. *Josh* mein these things happen, you know. Young blood is very hot. But in your *josh*, don't give up something you will regret later on. Boys like Bunty don't grow on trees . . ."

I turned to Dad in despair. He was his usual laissez-faire self. "Let it be, Lalitha. *Zamana badal gaya hai*, life is different today. She is a sensible girl. I am sure she will make the right decisions only," he said, putting his arm around me and giving me a hug. I hugged him back, hoping he would prove to be right.

35

A day before my flight, Mom got all excited about the trip and rushed to the nearby Tibetan market to bring back a giant white jacket which made me look and feel like a Yeti when I wore it reluctantly. But I couldn't refuse to take it and walked around trying to look as pleased about it as she did. In a way, I *was* pleased. The jacket was her way of supporting me and how could I not be pleased with her support? The jacket was like a visible embodiment of her love, an armour of her protection against the world on me. Of course, to keep the balance, she also casually passed on the tidbit that Bunty was in London too and that I should call him when I reached there. Yeah, right! Mothers never give up hope!

London was a blast. Though also very expensive. The hotel room I was staying in was 200 pounds per night (thank God my company was paying for it!) and yet it was a lot smaller than the ₹5000 room at the Ambassador in Bombay. The prices of everything in the city made my credit card leap back into my wallet with a frightened whimper.

The team I had to work with was really sweet and made me

feel right at home. Lizzie was a fast-talking, joke-a-minute type and was frighteningly good at her work. She also loved to party and promised to show me the London night life. Harry, her copy partner, had a typically British style of humour and was great fun. Both of them loved the campaign and we thought up all kinds of fun ways to extend the idea and to make it more British. The duo took me pub-hopping on the second day of my arrival, and out to Covent Garden for lunch the next day.

It was good to be away from Delhi and from the memories of Dhir and to be plunged in a completely different kind of life. Over the weekend, I did the tourist circuit—Madame Tussauds, where I had to get a picture with Mahatma Gandhi for Mom, the hop-on hop-off tourist buses which have been featured in more Hindi movies than the number of buses themselves, 221B Baker Street and the Tower of London. Liz and Harry took me out clubbing on Saturday night to Annabel's, the 'it' spot for London's high-fliers.

Interestingly, the club had a DJ who mixed in Hindi film and bhangra numbers after every few songs and these rocked so much that the whole bar would get emptied out when he played them, as everyone would rush to the dance floor to perform their own version of desi bhangra. Cultural colonisation, I thought to myself with a laugh. There were lots of BBCD types there and I found it fascinating to hear them speak in impeccable British accents with all the modern slangs thrown in. Back in India, when you do find someone with a Brit accent, their language tends to be fossilised, like that of Roshan Seth, or of any other plummy-voiced stage actor for that matter.

Liz and Harry had told me that even Princes William and Harry party there, so I was keeping a weather eye out. Nothing like a royal fling to get over a break-up! Suddenly I saw a guy who looked like Bunty. I concentrated through the red-blue-green lighting-and-strobe flashes and realised to my horror that it was actually Bunty! God! I needed to hide; I carefully maneuvered my Guinness bottle in front of my face. But it was unnecessary, because Bunty was ensconced in a cozy corner on a plush suede sofa, playing tongue-hockey with someone. Hmm, interesting, I thought, considering he is allegedly recovering from heartbreak. I craned my neck to see who he was with, and then almost had a heart attack!

He was smooching Miklos!

That got me all steamed up. Why had he put me through that freak show at the railway station when he was interested in batting for the opposite team? I sneakily took a couple of pictures of him using my new cellphone. Now I had my ammo if Mom were to ever bring up the topic of Bunty again!

A week later, the campaign work all wrapped up, I headed back to Delhi, bags weighed down with Pimm's and sherry bottles. I was dying to tell Mom all about Bunty. London had given me a juicier piece of gossip and a sharper revenge than anything I could have dreamed up on my own.

But somehow, when Mom grilled me on whether I had called and met Bunty while in London, I just said no (Mom heaved a deep disappointed sigh) and didn't indulge in any goss.

"Neera Auntie is really upset, you know. Bunty took your

refusal very hard. Poor boy! He is such a sweet boy, became very depressed by what happened with you."

I had to get to the bottom of this, so I called him up.

"Hi, Bunty."

"Who's this?"

"Kajal. You don't have my number saved?"

"No, actually something's wrong with my phone's display. Not able to see who's calling." His voice had gone from peppy to doleful.

"Hmmm. Bunty, I felt really bad about running out on you . . . I've been wanting to talk to you . . . Can we meet up?"

"Oh, ummm, I'm a little busy right now . . ."

"Well, it's important. Should I come over to your place or do you want to meet somewhere outside?"

He agreed to meet up at a nearby TGIF. I guess he noticed the won't-give-up tone of my voice.

"So, Bunty, how have you been?"

"Ok, I guess." Bunty had turned up with a hangdog expression and unshaven face, but I wasn't buying any of it.

"Mom said you were really upset about what happened . . ."

"Yeah . . . I guess I didn't expect to be . . . so brutally shot down . . . I mean you had been giving me all kinds of signals . . ."

"Bunty, the only signals I've ever given you are 'Stop' and 'No Entry'. Seriously, I have no idea when you got other signals."

"Well, I don't know about that Kajal . . . I really thought we were going somewhere."

I had just been messing with him, trying to see what he'd come up with. But this was beginning to get outrageous.

"So . . . I heard you were in London recently?"

"Yeah . . . I was really feeling down, so Mom suggested I take a holiday."

"Oh, really? What did you do there?"

"Nothing much . . . you know, I just couldn't get into anything because of . . . (sigh) . . . Well I don't want to bother you with the sad story."

Enough! If Bunty kept this up for five more minutes, he might be served up with green eggs. He was that big of a ham!

I took a deep draught of my LIIT. "I was in London last week. In fact I was there for a couple of weeks."

"Oh . . . how nice."

"Yes, and you know Londoners are so bold. I actually saw a gay couple making out one night at Annabel's."

"Oh, how shocking!" His voice sounded just a teensy bit shaky.

"No, that wasn't the shocking part. What shocked me was who it was I spotted." I pulled out my cellphone. Bunty had a hunted look on his face.

"See, that looks just like you, doesn't it? And he is kissing this guy who looks just like Miklos. But that can't be you, because you were so busy mourning me, right? I'm planning to psych Neera Auntie by pretending that's you. Don't you think that'll be funny?"

I shoved the cellphone in his face. I felt a bit mean but I was really riled. I'd had it with my mom's sympathy for Bunty and his growing rep as the local Devdas.

Bunty looked around the room as if hunting for inspiration, his eyes half out of their sockets. He gulped a couple of times.

"That . . . that's . . . not me . . ."

"I know. That's what'll make it so funny. I'm planning to email this to Mom tonight."

"No, no, please . . ."

"But why? It's just a joke."

"No . . . it'll kill my mom."

"Oh?"

Bunty sighed, and looked defeated. "Ok . . . that's me, I admit."

"So what is all this about? Clearly you weren't in mourning or denial or whatever . . . You were never even interested in me. So what gives?"

"My mom . . . she's been after me for years, 'Get married, get married!' She's constantly setting me up with one girl or another. And, lately, she and your mom have been getting increasingly serious about their plan of getting us married. I started feeling desperate. I mean I've known for years that I'm . . . umm . . . gay, but obviously I couldn't tell my folks that, especially after my cousin brother Dev came out two years ago. He lived with us during his college years *na*, so Mom keeps blaming herself, thinking she did something wrong to 'turn him gay'. So . . . I just came up with this plan. I thought . . . if I pretend to be heartbroken and stuff, everyone will stop pestering me . . . at least for a while . . ."

"Okay, but what if I'd fallen for you and your act?"

"Come on, Kajal, I knew there was no risk of that. Neither of us has ever felt the slightest interest in each other, even as human beings!"

I started laughing; it was true and refreshing to hear him say it.

"Oh stop, I might blush."

He laughed too at that but quickly turned serious again. "Please, Kajal. I know it's a huge favour to ask and I don't deserve it, but can you please keep my secret?"

"Relax, Bunty. I had no intention of telling anyone anything, anyway. I just wanted to get at the truth. But how long do you think you can keep it hidden from everyone?"

"All my life, if I have to. I just can't do this to my mom, you know. I'm not ashamed of being gay; it's just a fact of life. But she won't get it."

"How long have you been seeing Miklos?"

"We've been together for four years now. He was posted here to work at my company. He's from Ukraine but has lived in London most of his life. We've been living together for almost three years now."

"And no one knows?"

"Well, some of my friends do."

"It's amazing how you've been getting away with it."

"Well, you know landlords. They only suspect hanky-panky with the opposite sex, but they never think that two guys or girls could be a couple. So they just think we're sharing a flat. They don't know it's much more than that."

I deleted the pictures from my phone. I had never intended to out him anyway. I felt sorry for him. Not because he was gay but because he was going to have to live undercover all his life. He would never be able to share his life with his partner and keep his parents happy at the same time. And he'd have to face pressure about getting married all his life. At least, as and when I get my act together and find a partner, I would be able to introduce him to everyone I know and live with him openly. He'd be a part of my life, not tucked into a little corner, hidden away from the world.

I promised Bunty I'd back up his story of rejection and heartbreak. It wasn't going to hurt me and was only going to help him. We parted soon after, better friends than we'd ever been.

36

Work was going well and we were ready with the India campaign. We had roped in a minor starlet and a hot new model for the ad. We shot them in Pondicherry, which was a new and interesting location.

I finally told Shonali about breaking up with Dhir. She was in two minds about it. "I think you're mad! If you're so into him, you should give it a try. Come to Bombay, make it work out" was her first reaction, "But I don't know if *I* would be able to chuck my career and make a similar move. I've . . . kind of got a similar situation going on" was her second.

"Who? What? When did this happen?"

"Never mind, that's a long story. If there was anything to tell, I'd have spilled the beans. But . . . I think we've almost decided to call it off. Long distance doesn't work in this day and age; life moves too fast. Every single day, so much happens that if you don't share it on a ball-by-ball basis, you tend to lose track of where the other person is. And at the same time, I don't think I can just throw up everything I've worked so hard for and move."

In some ways, I feel Women's Lib has made life harder. Life was easier when one person had more choices, and the other one had, perforce, to follow. Once both people got the sanction and liberty to make choices, it became all too easy to feel two opposite pressures tugging one apart all the time.

Shonali heartened me by telling me that Dhir was suffering. Not that I really wanted him to suffer, but . . . it just felt good to know that he was as woebegone by our break-up as I was. I still felt we had an amazing connection and every time something funny or really good or really bad happened, I would almost instinctively pick up the phone to tell him about it. Once I even accidentally called him, out of sheer habit, but then hung up when I heard his voice.

The campaign finally broke in December and it worked better than our wildest dreams. Almost immediately, the media picked it up and ran stories and audience polls around it. Then they picked up some of the lines to use in their own stories about other things. For instance, there was some political hoo-hah between the partners in the ruling coalition, and HT captioned it in a cartoon with, "Not using Lucky?" Amul picked up the ads and did their butterly take on them. It soon became drawing-room conversation and the stuff of theme parties. The whole thing snowballed until people in the business started saying we'd surely get an Abby award for it, and that the Campaign of the Year award was definitely in the bag.

RKS was nice enough to let Junaki and me take all the credit for the campaign. We were even profiled in the 'Talents to Watch' section of the business press. When I visited Mom and Dad for Mom's birthday, I was both pleasantly and extremely surprised to find that Mom had cut all the press coverage to make a huge collage, displayed in the drawing room. All the UK press coverage was also included in the collage. Dad had surfed the net to pick it up. They'd even cut out the press ads and mounted them in frames. I was so emotional I couldn't speak and just hugged both of them tightly. "I always knew you'll make us proud, *beta*," Mom said, stroking my hair. "I'm sorry I acted so hyper about it."

Dad was beaming from ear to ear. "I always knew our *beti* is a *kamaal ki cheez* (I always knew our daughter is wonderful)."

Really, there's nothing on earth like one's parents.

I'd forgotten that Neera Auntie and Gappu Uncle's wedding anniversary was on the same day as Mom's birthday. They had planned a huge do and Mom and Dad were going. As usual, they dragged me along. "But, Mom, Neera Auntie hates me after I said no to Bunty," I protested.

"No, *beta*, nothing like that. She is just disappointed that she missed such a wonderful *bahu*, that's all. She's been bragging to everyone about your campaign."

Mom made me wear a *sari* she had picked up—pale green with *kundan*-style stone work on the border—and helped me tie my hair in a French Knot. I must admit I looked pretty good. I hadn't seen Bunty in weeks, having been tied up with the campaign, so I was looking forward to seeing him.

"Neera Auntie, Gappu Uncle, congratulations!"

"Thanks, *beta*, and congratulations to you too. Everybody's been talking about your campaign. You have done it very well," Auntie said with a warm smile. I smiled back, relieved that she had forgiven me.

I wandered off in search of liquid refreshment and people my own age. I finally spotted Bunty at the bar, scoffing down whisky.

"Hey, Bunty, what's up, man?"

"Nothing, *yaar*."

"Then why so sad? You're really looking down and don't tell me it's a part of the act for your parents' benefit."

"No, it's not that. It's Miklos. He wants us to come out with our relationship. He . . . I didn't invite him here today, and lately he's been upset about all the hiding and sneaking anyway. We've been arguing rather a lot lately, and yesterday I just left in a huff. He's planning to go back to the UK."

"Omigod. What are you going to do?"

"I don't know. I just can't do this to Mom, you know. But if I lose Miklos . . ."

Suddenly I spotted someone familiar in the crowd. "Isn't that him over there?"

Bunty turned and looked in the direction I was pointing. "Oh God, it is him!"

Despite his distress, I saw how Bunty's face all lit up on seeing Miklos. It was really too bad that convention was not going to let these two be together, I thought.

"Bunty, I'm sorry I barged in, but I couldn't stay away. I'm tired of all the running around, all the sneaking around. Either we're together or we're not. I can't be this little secret part of your life, as if I'm something to be ashamed of. Come on, Bunty, I love you. We love each other. Let's not treat it as something dirty and sordid."

Miklos hadn't waited to see whether the coast was clear

when he had started talking. So I was bang in the middle of their argument.

"Miklos . . . I agree with you in principle . . . but I can't do that to my parents. They'll never understand . . . And my mom . . . she's been wanting grandkids for years. It's something every mother in India looks forward to . . ."

"So what are you saying, Bunty? Are you going to marry someone else—her perhaps," Miklos jerked his thumb towards me, "and pretend to be happy? Have kids, lead a double life? Hide your truth from everyone? I'm sorry, Bunty, but I can't be a part of this . . . this lie. I have to be honest about who I am and what I am. Fine, you've made your choice. I'm going to take the first train out of here."

Miklos turned on his heel and walked away, leaving a tortured Bunty looking after him in shock. Bunty buried his face in his hands. "It's all over. My life is over. I can't deal with it without him. I won't be able to take it. I . . . I want to kill myself. I'm going to kill myself."

"Yeah, because that'll be easier for your Mom and Dad to bear than knowing that their son is gay, knowing that he killed himself. Don't be an ass, Bunty. Go after Miklos. You love him. And love doesn't walk in every day. You're lucky to have found it and you would be an idiot of the first order if you let it go. You have to make your own luck, you know that. Go after him, get him back right now. You can talk to your parents later, explain things to them. I'll help you speak to your parents. Come on."

Bunty looked shaken and palsied as we both walked to the exit gate. Then he suddenly shook my hand off his arm.

"Kajal, it's ok. I know what I have to do. I have to speak to my parents first. Make them understand. Then I'll go after Miklos. I don't want to do things half-heartedly any more. I want to get on the *ghodi* and go—you know, *sehra baandhkar*!"

I don't know what Bunty said or how he explained everything to his parents, but I am sure they must have been pretty confused about everything, considering that the story of him proposing to me and being broken-hearted thereafter must have been at the back of their minds. Somewhere, I think Neera Auntie never quite got it and remained convinced that my turning down Bunty had 'turned him gay'. Not that I cared, as long as they were all happy with the situation. No, I think 'happy' is too strong a word for what Neera Auntie and Gappu Uncle felt that day, but at least they both gave Bunty their blessings.

Gappu Uncle had organised a *shaadi ki ghodi* with all the trappings, since it was their thirty-fifth anniversary and he wanted to make a grand gesture. As soon as all three of them emerged from their confab, Bunty actually made good on what he said: he flung himself on the *ghodi* and galloped off to the station to find Miklos (the next train was only at midnight, so he was sure he'd find Miklos there). Most of the guests, in their touching naïveté, remained a little confused about what exactly was happening. And Neera Auntie somehow looked the most confused of them all. Mom was befuddled too, of course, even after Bunty came back with Miklos for his happy ending.

I returned to Delhi in a thoughtful mood. It seemed as if I didn't believe in anything I had told Bunty. Either that or

I didn't believe I loved Dhir. Otherwise how had I let other things—things that didn't matter, because there was a way around them—get in the way? I stewed over it for a week, and then I finally made my decision. I was going to move to Bombay and find Dhir, and hoped like hell he hadn't found someone else in the meantime. I was going to ask my boss for a transfer but, failing that, I'd just do a job hunt on reaching Bombay. I'd grabbed the bull by the horns in my professional life in the last few months and it was time for me to do the same in my personal life.

I toyed with the idea of calling up Dhir and informing him of my decision, but my fear got the better of me—fear that he might say he'd moved on or had changed his mind about us or that he didn't feel anything special any more. Of course, what I would do if he said that to my face later, I had no idea, but rational thinking isn't my strong suit anyway.

I told RKS about the transfer I wanted.

"We'll have to see what we can do, but it might take a while."

"I need to move by January. I'm moving to Bombay anyway on 1st Jan, so I'll need to know by then."

"But, Kajal, these things take time. It's not just my sole decision, you know."

"I'm sorry, RKS, but if it doesn't work out by then, I'll start job-hunting there."

"Ok, what is all this about? Why the sudden move and the hurry?"

I told RKS all about Dhir and what I had been going through (omitting certain personal details, of course).

"Wow, you've got balls. Ok, done. I'll manage your transfer. We don't want to lose a bright spark like you to the competition now, do we? And you'll have to promise to name your first-born after me, ok?"

37

My flying out on 1st Jan was kind of like a New Year's resolution. *Be Brave. Just Do It.* Junaki was going to move into my flat, since my lease was till April and she wanted to get out of her hellhole apartment. I packed up my few belongings and explained the move to Mom and Dad as best I could. Luckily, after the campaign and the Bunty episode, Mom was a lot less hyper about my decision-making abilities; Dad was his usual supportive self. He even managed to arrange a decent guest house at Nariman Point. I was planning to stay there for the first few weeks while I found a place for myself.

Debu the Incommunicado, showed up at my doorstep on New Year's Eve. I hadn't seen him for weeks and had been dying to tell him everything that had been going on. I was going to miss him like hell.

"Hi, stranger!"

"Hi, Kajal."

"Where have you been?"

"Oh, here and there."

"Listen, you moron, you've been gone so much, you're

practically not a part of my life any more. Idiot. Do you even know I'm moving to Bombay tomorrow?"

"What? How come?"

"I decided at long last that you were right about Dhir. It *was* special and I'd be stupid to let it die like this. You know how sometimes you buy flowers and then forget to change the water and they just droop? That's what we've done to our relationship, Dhir and I. But I need to know if the flowers will revive if we start watering them again. So I'm shifting to Bombay. I got a transfer from the company."

"Wow, guess who's been doing some growing up!"

"Yeah, can't be sixteen forever, I guess. So, anyway, I'm done packing and all I have left here is some serious booze. I don't feel much like partying today. Are you doing something tonight?"

"No . . ."

"So come on over later and we can have a last knees-up, relive the good times and all . . . I'm really going to miss you, you know . . ."

"Well, I don't know about that."

"Which, coming over or missing you?"

"Both. You see, I have some news of my own."

"Yeah . . .?"

"I'm moving out of Delhi, too."

"Really? Where to? Why? When did *this* happen?"

"I'm moving to Bombay."

I flung myself on him, giving him a big hug.

"Wow! How great is this! That is so cool. Maybe we can be roomies? I heard apartment rentals are ruinous in Bombay."

For the first time, he cracked a smile and said, "I doubt if that'll be possible. You see, I'm moving in with Shonali."

I had to shake my head like a dog to make sure I was hearing properly. "What? Who? When? How?"

"It started when she was in Delhi."

"But I thought you guys couldn't agree on anything. I thought you drove each other nuts!"

"We did, but in a good way. I've been going back and forth to Bombay, working long distance. She's not ready to move here, so I figured since I could easily work from anywhere, I'd take the plunge."

"Great! But you guys are such goons! Why didn't you tell me something was going on?"

"We've been going back and forth about it ourselves—like you and Dhir—but you are the first person to know!"

"I'm so happy for you both! This is so great! Hey, now we all can hang out in Bombay!"

"Yup. And I have to say, kiddo, I think you're being gutsy. I'm sure it'll work out. But . . . about tonight . . . a no will have to do. Shonali's flying in."

"Ok. See if you lovebirds want to drop in for a bit. Shit, I'm so psyched about this. It's going to be great!"

I was really kicked to think my two best friends had gotten together and that they'd both be in Bombay. It seemed like the move to Bombay was really meant to be. Everything was falling into place.

I sat out on my balcony, enjoying the freezing cold breeze, with the music of Nusrat playing on the mini-stereo I was planning to leave for Junaki. Delhi winters—I was really going to miss them in Bombay. I could smell the smoke of a hundred bonfires rising into the air and see the twinkling lights of traffic far below. I had finally popped open the bottle of champagne the agency had given me at the farewell party. No occasion could be more appropriate for champagne than my coming of age. I felt like I was finally on my way to adulthood, taking chances, realising that nothing in life comes with guarantees and that what was important was to keep trying.

The doorbell rang close to midnight and I sprang up to answer it, expecting to see Shonali and Debu, come to ring in the New Year. I flung the door open, a broad grin on my face, saying, "You two really owe me big time!" And then I ground to a halt.

It wasn't them; it was Dhir, as large as life.

We both stared at each other for the longest time. I had a funny, quivering feeling in the pit of my stomach. I tried to speak but no voice came out. I must have looked like a moron, pointing and gesturing, mouth opening and closing like a fish.

"What . . . what are you doing here?" A quavery whisper finally made its way out.

"I wanted to see you. Can we do this inside or we gotta do it in the hallway?"

I cracked the door open wider, gesturing him to come in. He looked wonderful, in a black jacket, red tee and a pair of blue jeans. I wished I was dressed in something other than a pair of Bugs Bunny pyjamas and a torn sweater. I'd been packing all day and my hair was piled up in an untidy bun atop my head. Was I fated to have him always see me at my worst?

I shut the door, leaning on it for a moment, praying: Please, let this be what I think it is. Please let him have come to say that our break-up was a mistake. I turned to face him. And he began:

"K . . . I don't know if it's already too late in the day or not . . . but . . . the past few months . . . I've been miserable. It's not working without you in my life . . . I think it's crazy—the way we met and how little time we've actually spent together—but I know that this is the most important thing that's ever happened to me and I don't want to give up on it. I just can't get you off my mind. I find it weird that I'm not talking to you every night, telling you about everything that happened to me during the day, or listening to you telling me about your day. I miss our arguments, our flirting, your jokes . . . I just signed off the biggest deal of my life today, and the first thing I wanted to do, even before the ink was dry, was call you. And then I remembered we'd broken up . . . I took the first flight I could get and flew here . . . I don't know if you're still free, if you're still even interested . . . but . . . I love you . . . I want this to work out . . . I want us to be together . . ."

He looked at me, eyes uncertain. My heart was so full, my eyes welled up. I did something I've only ever seen in movies. I ran to him and threw my arms around him. "Yes . . . yes . . . Oh my God, yes . . ."

It was as if I was watching a movie in slow motion: Dhir's lips came closer to mine ever so slowly . . . my heart was pounding so loud I thought it would be audible . . . a thousand baby butterflies were waltzing through my body . . . I felt like I was the champagne, and the cork exploded out of the bottle when his lips finally settled on mine . . .

Much, much later, when our heartbeats had approached something close to normal again, we both clinked our champagne glasses together, huge grins on our faces. Unfortunately, the apartment was in no condition to entertain, so we were cuddled together on the *gaddi*, covered with my yeti jacket.

"Hang on, I just remembered something," Dhir said, and headed out of the front door, wrapping my *shawl* around his midriff. He was back a moment later, lugging two large suitcases. I looked at him, puzzled, "What's this? Christmas gifts?"

"No . . . this is all my stuff. Well, except for the heavy things like the TV and the music system. I guess I could get one of my pals to send them to me later."

"Send them? Where?"

"Here."

"What? Why?"

"Kajal, didn't you hear me? I said I really want to make us work, so I'm moving here. This is all my stuff. I'll talk to my boss on Monday, because I'm sure he's out partying tonight. I did send him an SMS with my resignation though, on my way here. I will figure something out in Delhi . . . I've been thinking of starting my own business and Delhi's as good a place to do it as Bombay."

I started laughing.

"What's so funny?"

"See that—in the corner."

"Yeah . . . suitcases . . . I see them . . . so?"

"Don't you find my place a little bare? Doesn't it look a little more Siberia-ish since the last time you saw it?"

Dhir looked around, puzzled. There were bare spots on the wall from frames I had pulled down. There were no drapes on the windows; the cushions were without covers. But, like a typical male, Dhir shook his head.

I cupped his face between my hands. "I'm packed and I was to fly to Bombay tomorrow. I'd come to the same conclusion about us as you did. I was hoping to come, find you in Bombay and make pretty much the same speech you just did. You just beat me to the punch line!"

Epilogue

Well, it's a year later, and Dhir and I are very much together. In fact, we're getting married on 5th January next year, the second anniversary of the day we met. My folks love him and couldn't be happier to welcome him into the family. Since my transfer was through, I moved to Bombay. I'm now a Creative Director myself and supervise a team of three copywriters at work. Dhir finally started his e-business six months ago. We live in a tiny little hen-coop in the back of beyond. Life is pretty hectic but it's great!

Debu and Shonali have turned completely bohemian. Right after our wedding, they're taking off for a backpacking trip around the world. They don't even know when they're coming back. Wild, isn't it?

Bunty and Miklos are still together and are planning to perform an item number at my *sangeet*! They moved to London four months ago, because they wanted to get married, though they're flying in for my wedding. Neera Auntie and Gappu Uncle have finally come to terms with the fact that their son is gay, especially after Miklos and Bunty started planning their wedding. Of course, Neera Auntie isn't sure if she's the mother of the bride or the groom!